To give himself time
by BRADFORD PRATT

It's pouring, pouring white sand, clean every tooth better. "

Veronica slowly washed off the traces of a night hunt. Abrasions on the arms and legs were pinching from the water. She stood in the shower for a long time, but she did not manage to get rid of the sensation that she brought from night hunting and which, it seems, took root in her during the night, was saturated with new strength from her dreams. Nothing proved that the nightly events had even the slightest relation to breaking into her apartment. Nevertheless, Veronica did not let go of the thought that these events were connected. That something is happening that she does not understand. Some kind of hide and seek with obscure rules, so Veronica does not know who and where she should look. And is it even worth starting the search.

Fingers stroked the scar on the arm below the elbow. The skin on it was lighter and a little denser than around. I wonder how the body heals itself. Makes the damaged area stronger than before. The body learns from mistakes, unlike the brain.

Veronica wiped herself, pulled on linen, jeans and a long-sleeved T-shirt. She combed her hair in her tail and began to quietly go down the stairs. The clock was the beginning of the eighth.

The car started up on the second attempt. Fog lay above the crop fields, curled over the gravel path and around the spotlights. At the turn on the big road, she noticed a rickety shield, which she had not noticed yesterday. The logo of the enterprise that supplied the blades to wind farms. She recalled: the same logo was on documents on her father's desk.

On the way, Veronica looked closely at the windmills, which she passed by. The same logo. The blades spun barely, as if the giants had just woken up.

Veronica stopped the car on the path in front of the church. The thick church fence, covered with white stucco, looked like a rosary wall, but was three times lower.

It was almost complete calm. The tops of tall trees moved slightly, protecting the dead from the flat wind. Strands of fog crawled along the cemetery path, intensifying the smell of boxwood, suggesting a funeral. Veronica went around the white building of the church. In a few hours, the service will begin. Veronica thought of the grinning goat head on the ceiling. Is she there yet? And, actually, where would she go?

Grandmother and grandfather on the father's side rested in the same grave: an inconspicuous stone in the middle of the row. No wonder. The Nilson family did not like to stand out. But her mother's parents were completely different. Own plot, fifteen, if not twenty square meters, surrounded by a neat border. At the head of the head is a large tombstone of ferrous metal. The Aronson family tomb appeared on it in gold letters - it must have been that Uncle Harald recently ordered them to be refurbished. Among the carefully loosened coarse gravel, three gravestones were darkening: under them were the parents of his grandfather, his unmarried sister, and he and his grandmother. Landowner Assar Aronson. His wife Alva.

Mom's tombstone was a little off, near the cemetery wall. He was carved out of a pinkish, shiny rock whose name Veronica had forgotten.

Magdalena Nilson, nee Aronson

August 21, 1948 – December 18, 1983

On both sides of the grave rose bushes, flawlessly trimmed. A bush of white and a bush of red roses, as in the garden. Dad must have been here several times a week.

Under the name of the mother, his name was already inscribed.

Ebbe nilson

April 3, 1945 -

The date of death was not yet available. But his gaze did not linger on this empty place, but on the void under the names of the parents. There should have been a name for Billy. About ten years ago, someone hinted that it would finally be necessary to officially announce the death of the child, but the father instantly became furious that it was not common with him. Mother should not lie next to an empty coffin! Since then, no one dared to talk about it, even Uncle Harald.

Sorrow absorbs a person completely; then an acute mental pain passes into something that is easier to bear. The human psyche always tries to find bright moments even in the deepest darkness. He seeks a straw of hope, clings to it with all his might. It was this hope that ruined my mother. While Billy's body was not found, there remained hope and questions. Where is Billy now? What is he doing? Who pokes a blanket for my boy in the evenings, who comforts him when he cries?

Doctors treating Mom's depression claimed she was on her way to recovery. Veronica also suspected that her mother simply reconciled. I realized that there would be no answers. That only stones, ice and a lake will make you hope to leave her alone.

Veronica squatted near the grave. She cleared her throat, thinking over what to say.

- Hello, mom, it's me. - Veronica was struck by how stupid it sounded: the words came out awkward, as if someone had spoken them. When the mother was alive, they never had confidential conversations, and the attempt of sincerity here and now seemed like a cinematic cliche.

Veronica got up, ashamed, cleaned the pebbles from the legs. She really wanted to smoke, and she regretted that she had not shot yesterday a couple of cigarettes from Matthias.

Then Veronica noticed some small object on the stove - at first she did not pay attention to him. A black pebble, completely flat and smooth, as if waves had been grinding it for thousands of years. Veronica rolled him in the palm of her hand. It was not dad who put him here, she was sure of that. The stone appeared here recently, otherwise the father would have probably removed it: the stone broke perfect symmetry.

The morning feeling returned, even intensified. Something is happening here. In addition, another sensation began to grow in Veronica's soul: it was as if a pebble in her hand was feeding him with her energy.

Yes, something is happening here, and it's time to figure out what exactly.

Veronica walked quickly to the car. When she stepped out of the gate, for a brief, unpleasant moment, she thought that someone was standing at the corner of the church, she almost felt someone's gaze in her head. But when she turned around, the cemetery was empty, only two magpies, crackling, took off from a tall tree.

Food opened at exactly eight. Plastic floor, fluorescent lamps. The walls and ceiling have long been in need of repair. The aroma of fresh pastries from the bread department at Veronica rumbled loudly in her stomach. But the desire to smoke defeated hunger, and curiosity only intensified. If she is lucky, she will be able to satisfy both.

- Oh my God! Vera, is that you?

Aunt Berit went around the cash desk to hug her. Mom's classmate. And the best friend, as Berit herself claimed, but Veronica was sure that her mother would not agree with her.

Berit looked about as usual. A little more gray hair, a little heavier body, several new wrinkles around the mouth. Comfortable shoes, practical clothes, a voluminous red jacket with a store logo on the chest. She was fifty-five, as her mother would be now, but she looked a couple of years younger - a rarity in the village. Aunt Berit was one of those who say, until the air runs out, such people have to chop off every phrase with a breath.

"Lord, you haven't been here for five years." Or even longer, yeh?

Berit was married to Uncle Seren - a powerful man with a beard framing his face, an uneven bite and soft eyes; he was like an actor from those who play the good dad in television series. Søren often popped them with Mattias for ice cream when they came shopping, probably to get the opportunity to talk with their mom. Three generations of his family owned a grocery store, which meant that he himself, Berit, and their two children were not called by the Torgash as anyone, although of course they also had a surname - Möller. So it is here. For this or that resident of the village, the shadows of his parents and grandparents always loom. Søren and Berit-Torgashi. Eric the Carpenter. Sven Postman, Inger Seamstress. Veronica herself has always been Vera, the daughter of Ebbe and Magdalena, and it does not matter what is written in her driver's license or any other document.

In just a few minutes, Aunt Berit managed to tell the most significant. How she feels (well, despite all sores, inhale). How are her children, about whom Veronica remembered only that their names begin with L (also good). The boy, Luddy (that's what his name is), lives in Trelleborg, his sister Lena is still in the village. Both, of course, have several children.

They also managed to discuss the fact that Veronica did not have children (what a pity) or even a man (you just have not yet met the right person). Instead of upsetting Aunt Berit and asking questions herself, Veronica smiled sadly and muttered something, agreeing. Because Vera Nilson, daughter of Ebbe and Magdalena, should behave this way.

- Have you seen your uncle? Asked Aunt Berit. Veronica shook her head:

- Not yet.

"Well, yes, he's so busy, with new windmills."

Veronica said nothing, waiting for the continuation, and it followed.

"Ninety meters high, can you imagine?" We did not say anything when he put the former, but these new ones are almost twice as high. Machines that will be seen and heard from everywhere. The whole village is fucked up.

Aunt Berit shook her head and looked around quickly, as if to make sure no one was eavesdropping.

- And not only I think so. They are talking about challenging a building permit. Dad didn't say anything about this?

Veronica shook her head again.

"Well, yes, it is unlikely that Ebbe will rush to tell you about windmills first thing." You are so rarely at home.

- Right. - Veronica swallowed this poorly hidden rebuke. She tried to figure out how to find out what interests herself.

Aunt Berit seemed to be waiting for words that would give her the opportunity to continue talking about Uncle Harald's wind power, but she did not wait and left this topic. Her voice softened.

"You look more and more like your mother." The same beauty.

Veronica understood that this was a compliment, but she still did not like him.

Aunt Berit sighed.

"Magda was also a restless soul." You're all in it.

And an elderly woman, to Veronica's surprise, stroked her head. Regarding this gesture as her chance, Veronica decided to use it and asked:

- So mom and fled to Copenhagen? Restless soul pushed?

The question seemed to catch Aunt Berit by surprise. She squeezed her lips, straightened her jacket, hesitated, but still could not resist the temptation to portray her best friend.

"Your grandfather ..." Aunt Berit paused for a moment, searching for suitable words. - In general, Assar and your mother did not get along very well. Magde on the farm was not very comfortable. It's not that ... - Hitch again. Apparently, Aunt Berit did not know too much. Veronica understood this already by what she called mom Magda. Mother hated being called that. Veronica decided to push the conversation in the right direction.

"But then mom returned home," she prompted. "She married dad."

Aunt Berit nodded.

- Ebbe fell in love with Magda at school. Most of the boys were crazy about her. Except my Seren, of course, "she added hastily, which is why her words were not very reliable. "Unlike the other guys, Ebbe didn't even try to invite her anywhere." He was too shy, kept behind everyone. But it was enough to see how Ebbe was looking at Magda to understand how things were going. He idolized your mother, he was ready for anything for her.

Veronica mumbled something. That her father idolized such a treasure as mother was not news to her. We should arm ourselves with patience and carefully push the conversation towards the summer of 1983.

"We were terribly surprised when Magda suddenly showed up again at home," Aunt Berit continued. "It all happened so fast." Engagement, wedding, the birth of Matthias ...

Berit smiled wryly, and Veronica felt herself boiling. She heard these rumors. That dad is not Mattias's father. That Mom got pregnant from someone in Copenhagen and that Harald's grandfather and uncle brought her home and married her to avoid shame. Veronica even understood where these rumors came from. Matthias is a cut above his father, he has wide shoulders, powerful arms and facial features sharp, like that of Uncle Harald. You have to try hard to find something from dad in him. But Veronica knew: paternal features of the brother-in-law also exist.

She put her hand in the back pocket of her jeans, felt for a sheet of paper, realized that it was a photobot ... For a few seconds the women were silent.

Veronica felt herself wandering in the dark. She still does not really know what or whom she is looking for. However, a key character has already been identified throughout this story. A man who almost certainly knows the truth about Billy. Veronica decided to go straight to the point.

"Tommy Root," she said. This name, as Veronica calculated, frightened Aunt Berit. "You did know him, didn't you?"

Berit pulled her jacket back and looked around as if afraid that they were eavesdropping. There were no buyers yet, and the passion for gossip prevailed.

"Well, as I knew." We studied together - he, me and Magda. Seren, Ebbe and your uncle too. Tommy was cute, but no one loved him. Unpleasant type, unpredictable - drank, rowdy. She pursed her lips, and the wrinkles became clearer. - Once he cracked my Seren on the head with a bottle. In the People's Park. We were sixteen to seventeen years old. It could end very badly. Tommy molested the girls, and Søren intervened. He had eight stitches, but we still did not report to the police.

- Why?

Aunt Berit shook her head.

- Father Tommy came home to Seren's parents with a whole deer, as a patch for wounds. He was not the first time to clean up after his boyfriend. And soon after that, Tommy went to sea. They chatted as if before he had beaten his own father.

Veronica tried to keep a serious and sympathetic expression on her face. She remembered a photograph of Tommy Roth in a newspaper. A heavy, dangerous look. Veronica tried to imagine how Root was glued to seventeen-year-old Aunt Berit, but nothing came of it.

"Uncle Seren was probably the last person to see Roth after ..." She left the phrase hanging in the air, and Aunt Berit immediately swallowed the bait.

- Yes. On the highway that leads south that evening that the police released him. Directly to Telleborg, and there by ferry - and abroad. He drove his eerie red "Volvo" as if the devils were chasing him. She snorted contemptuously. "What a shame that Monson could not keep Roth locked up." That Root never got punished for what he did to Billy.

This name made Aunt Berit stop the torment. She cringed and began nervously sorting through the packages of coffee on the shelf. She seemed suddenly terribly carried away by the layout of the goods. The topic was slippery, and Veronica understood that Aunt Berit could apologize at any time and say that she needed to work. And Veronica made her last attempt to find out what she did not know yet.

"Did anyone in the village talk to Root?"

Aunt Berit shook her head, once more aligned the bags.

"Only this one, well, another drunkard."

- A drunkard?

Aunt Berith turned to her. With a sharp gesture, as if wishing to get rid of something unpleasant, invisible, but tenacious, she shook off her jacket.

"Chell-Oke Ulson," she muttered. - Nicknamed Sailor.

Chapter 35

Veronica stood in front of the grocery, angrily tore up a cellophane on a pack and was about to smoke a "Prince" when a big black BMW with tinted windows taxied directly to her. The door opened, and a figured woman, the same age as Veronica, got out of the car.

- I thought that I was not mistaken. Vera!

It turned out to be Lydia, her classmate, whom Veronica had not seen for about ten years, or even more - fortunately, they managed to get around this sensitive issue. Lydia almost did not change with age. Pretty, well-dressed. High heels, pantsuit. Hair styled, flawless manicure on long nails. Both she and her expensive car did not fit well with the village, but Lydia did not seem to pay attention to it. She spoke loudly, and laughed even louder.

"By the way, Vera, did you have breakfast?"

- Uh, no ...

- And I'm just going to dad. Come with me, he will be terribly happy with you.

Veronica began to dissuade, but Lydia interrupted her, not allowing to disperse. In addition, Veronica forgot to buy food. Therefore, she got into her decrepit car and drove behind Lydia's chic BMW. She herself was surprised at her spontaneous decision. Somehow not like her. On the other hand, all this morning was, to put it mildly, unlike ordinary ones. Veronica never got rid of the strange feeling that visited her in the cemetery, and what to do with it until she knew.

They parked near one of the pizzerias on the outskirts of the village, with the sign "The right to sell alcohol" at the entrance. Veronica remembered Lydia's father, Branko, a big noisy man, one of those who, in the sixties and seventies, got here by bus from Yugoslavia to revive Swedish industry. Branco has now lost a lot of weight, but remains just as noisy.

"Gastroshunting," he laughed and patted his stomach. "I dropped forty-five kilos." Forty-five - count half Lydia.

- Well dad! - Lydia rolled her eyes, after which she kissed her father on both cheeks.

Branko invited them to sit down and, although it was still very early, put up a mountain of everything on the table.

"Protests won't help," Lydia whispered. "Just try and he will be satisfied."

Veronica, to the delight of Branco, filled her plate. He shouted to some of the employees some words that were not clear to her and also sat down at the table.

"Good to see you, Vera," he said. - Like Dad? For a long time he didn't come in.

- Thank you, good. - Veronica was surprised. Does dad eat pizza? He always preferred to cook on his own. And cooked well. "Did Lydia tell me?" She's capable of directly Rockefeller ... - Dad, that's enough. - Lydia tried to squeeze her father's mouth.

Both were jokingly bickering for some time, and Veronica felt an awkward smile crawl across her face. She tried to imagine her own father here. - He just wants to say that I have my own company, and things are going well. Hair products, lotions, perfumes. - Right here, in the Rafting? - Veronica herself heard how much surprise in her voice. - So what? Rafting is a great place. Low rent, lots of labor. We have a page, customers order goods online. My girls pack and mail. We have customers all over the country.

Lydia's father shook his head. - I also learn this, I get into all sorts of interns. Lydia says yes. God knows. The old dog will not teach new tricks. "I won't learn new tricks, that's right." And the old dog can very well learn, if he does not want to dangle into the city every time he needs to settle something in the bank.

They again argued in jest, and Veronica turned away and began to examine the photographs on the wall. Completely pictures of guests; on one, to her surprise, she recognized her father. He had more hair, and the photo faded slightly - apparently, he was ten years old. Dad was sitting at the table with a man and raised a beer mug into the cell. The man was partially covered by his father's right hand. Veronica did not recognize him.

"... a nail salon," Lydia said, and Veronica realized that she was negotiating some kind of phrase. - I already have two, but in a few years I will get a franchisee in every shopping center throughout Skane. Fast Nails. It will be cool, honestly.

"Great," said Veronica. She involuntarily looked at the photograph of her father. He looked joyful, but his eyes, as always, were sad.

"By the way, Branko," she said when she was about to leave. "Do you know Chell-Oke Ulson, nicknamed Sailor?" - She asked the question on a hunch, she herself did not know what answer awaited.

- Of course. Sailor was a regular here until he went nuts. He was forced out of the tavern ... - Branko waved his hand, as if he didn't like his own story.

- They forced it out?

- Yes, or how to say it right? He snapped his fingers, searching for the right word. - They stopped noticing him, here. No one wanted to drink with him. Say-lor said he was spat on beer.

"Because he knew Tommy Root?"

- Surely. - Branko crooked. - People here are vindictive. This is bad. Life is too short.

If your father has nothing against Sailor, then I am even more so. - My father?

Veronica noticed that Lydia quietly pulled Branco by the sleeve, but he did not let himself be knocked down. "Ebbe and Sailor were friends." Sometimes they drank a glass. Here look. - Branko went to that same photograph on the wall and pointed to the man sitting next to his father. - This is sailor.

Chapter 36

The nursing home was located at the eastern end of the village, not far from the church. Veronica was here for the last time since her grandfather's life on his father's side. Fifteen years ago or more - what's the difference, actually? Now we need to think about something else. The printout remained in the back pocket. Veronica put her hand in there, gently touched the paper.

In the nursing home, the smell of coffee spilled over gray linoleum. Rigid, heavy-looking wooden furniture stood in the corridors where they were expanding slightly. Like some paintings from a peasant manor that hung on the walls, she got here from a past life. Few people need clumsy things from another time. So you can say about ProSailor.

Already by the tone of the nurse, Veronica realized that Sailor is not particularly loved here. He sat behind a closed door in his room, in a wheelchair; on his knees - a plaid, although it was not less than twenty-five degrees of heat. Withered, bent body. The nose and cheeks are covered with a net of bursting blood vessels - a pattern well known to Veronica: she saw this in alcoholics who came to group psychotherapy.

"Here are your guests, Chell-Oke." Great, huh?

Nurse Maria is a school friend. Veronika remembered the name, only furtively looking at the badge, but she recognized it in her face right away. Maria seems to have agreed that Sailor is a longtime friend of Veronica's father, although doubt glanced in her gaze.

Sailor looked unfriendly at Mary, then at Veronica. His lower lip slanted obliquely, a lump of white mucus gathered in the corner of his mouth. His lips moved slightly, a faint, dull sound was heard.

"My name is Vera Nilson," said Veronica.

It was strange to pronounce this name. Still would. Her name has long been different.

"The daughter of Ebbe and Magdalena," she added: Sailor did not show that he recognized her. - From Bakkagorden. You were friends with my father.

The name of the farm made the old man raise his head. A light lit in his eyes, but Sailor continued to be silent. His gaze wandered between her and the nurse. Veronica turned to Mary, making it clear that she could handle it herself, but she misinterpreted everything.

- I told you - Chell-Oke has dementia. There is not much left of him. He is here and there.

- I see. - Veronica stared at Mary; she finally dismantled her hint.

"Well, I have to go, you'll probably manage it yourself." - A slight discontent was heard in the nurse's voice. She seemed to want to linger for another minute. - Chell-Oke is sometimes a little noisy and dissolves his tongue, but this is not dangerous. If anything, ring the bell. And keep in mind: we will pick him up soon, we'll take him to feed him.

Veronica waited until the sound of Maria's Birkenstocks sandals calmed down, dragged her chair and sat down next to Sailor. He smelled faintly of urine and something sweet - Veronica did not want to know what exactly.

"You were friends with Tommy Root," she set to work, not even trying to start a small talk. Sailor's eyes narrowed.

"You are Aronson's daughter," hissed half, he muttered half.

"Niece," she corrected. "Harald is my uncle."

"Fucking bitch," Sailor said. Then he turned his gaze inward, and the evil expression disappeared from his face. Senile fingers fingered the plaid.

"You and Tommy had things in common." Hunt, "Veronica reminded.

The last word made Sailor cringe. Anger returned to him.

- Shit. For everyone. Curious bastards. I will not say anything. Our business. Mine and Tommy. Aronson is a fucking bitch.

"So you and Tommy did not love my uncle?"

The old man looked up at her.

- Aronson fucking bitch.

- Yes, you already said.

Veronica sat waiting for the continuation, but Sailor stubbornly pursed his lips. Veronica made a new call.

"You and Tommy were hunting together in the North Forest, right?" Although it was my uncle's land.

Sailor leaned forward, grinned.

- May be. May be. Tommy. Maybe the forest, maybe ... - The look went out again, the fingers began to look for something on the plaid.

Veronica sighed. It was impossible to talk with the old man, completely pointless. What did she expect from this visit? What would Sailor explain to her who slipped into her father's garden or laid a stone on her mother's grave? Is it he who can only move from his room to the dining room and back?

From the street came the ringing of a church bell calling for service. This means that on Sundays the second breakfast for the elderly is about eleven.

Veronica tried in vain to figure out what else to say. She was ready to get up and leave when she suddenly decided something. She even caught her breath from the familiar sensation that appeared. She sat back in her chair and studied Sailor intently. His gaze and how he goes over the plaid. The smallest changes on his face.

"You're sad," she said softly. "You grieve for your friend, yes, Chell-Oke?"

Sailor did not answer. He was still looking at his own knees, but his fingers froze, stopped sorting through the fabric.

"Was Tommy a good friend?" - asked Veronica. The old man was silent, but it seemed to her that he nodded weakly.

"Have you been a good friend to him, Chell-Oke?"

This time the nod was clearer.

"I helped Tommy when he went to sea for the first time." He was so young. I taught him, looked after him. - Sailor was silent.

Veronica acutely regretted that there was no notebook with her.

"So Tommy was a good friend?" She repeated. Sailor looked at her. His eyes flashed.

"A good friend will not betray," he said sullenly. - Never. Tommy
did not betray. Until that summer.

"So you think Tommy betrayed you?" Abandoned?

Sailor lowered his eyes again.

"Listen, you were defending Tommy." You were a good friend,
and he left you. Left alone with people who were angry with him for
what he did, they were angry with you for knowing him. - Veronica
fell silent, wanting to make sure that Sailor was listening to her.

"I was Tommy a good friend," muttered Sailor. - good.

"He no longer spoke of himself?" After that summer? - Veronica
held her breath.

- Not. - Sailor shook his head. - Not a word ...

Veronica forced herself to wait, not to interrupt him with
questions.

"He got what he deserved," Sailor said suddenly. The voice
became sharp.

- Who? Tommy?

- Not! Aronson I got what I deserve. He didn't have to fit in ...
Deprived Tommy of a piece of bread. Tommy and his family. And
Tommy did it. Tommy ... - The words seemed to be stuck with
Sailor halfway between the brain and mouth. A wandering gaze
filled with alarm. Veronica took a deep breath.

"What did Tommy do?" She asked.

The old man's lips splashed wet against each other. He seemed to
be unsuccessfully searching for an answer.

"What did Tommy do with my little brother?"

"Out of the bush," the old man said.

- What a hut?

- Askedalen. Hunting Tommy is not to blame ... - The rest of the
sentence drowned in slurred mumble.

- Tell me about the hut. - Veronica leaned forward.

- To hell! - Sailor yelled suddenly so that a spray of saliva flew
into her face, forcing him to recoil. He began to swing back and
forth. - Mystery, hut - mystery. Why didn't you say anything,
Tommy? Why didn't you say how it was?

He suddenly fell silent and went limp. Fingers again began to sort
out the plaid.

- Chell-oke? - called Veronica. - Sailor?

She carefully laid a hand on his knee, but he did not respond. Veronica heard a quiet sound, as if someone was approaching the door in sandals.

Veronica guessed to get a printout; expanding the picture, she laid it on the old man's lap. Steps were coming. It seems that two were walking along the corridor. Sailor glanced at the image. Then to Veronica.

"Do you recognize him, Sailor?"

Voice, someone grabbed the doorknob. Veronica brought the photograph to the old man's face. Sailor looked away, as if something unpleasant was depicted on a sheet. His lips moved again.

"The truth is up there," he muttered. - Far in the forest, where no one will find. I told him so.

- To whom?

Door opened. Maria and another nurse stood at the door.

"It's time, Chell-Oke."

Veronica pulled the picture to herself, to fold it and put it in her pocket, but her fingers slipped and the photo was on the floor. Maria bent to pick her up.

"Ah, so you know Kitty?"

- Whom?

- Kitty, Isaka. Well, we called him that. Saylor's nephew. She shook the printout lightly and turned it so that her colleague looked too.

"Hasak been here?" - Stomach brought. - When?

- About a month ago. You won't forget it soon. Do you understand what I mean? - Maria winked at her, after which she turned to Sailor. - Well, Chell-Oke, let's go to the dining room. Today cabbage rolls, your beloved.

The old man smiled broadly. There was no trace of the previous anxiety on his face. Veronica already wanted to get up, but when the nurse took the arms of the chair and removed it from the brake, Sailor reached for Veronica and squeezed her fingers.

"Thank you for listening, Vera," he suddenly said distinctly. - Say hello to dad. Tell what...

Sailor hesitated, as if he had lost the thread again. He continued to squeeze her hand with his thin old fingers, as if not wanting to let go. - Say that? - Veronica out of the corner of her eye noticed how Maria bent to eavesdrop. The old man's voice was quiet, a little louder than a whisper. "Tell Ebbe that summer will end soon."

Chapter 37

A person remembers some moments of childhood better, others worse. Veronica still remembered the song The winner takes it all. ABBA broke up in January of the year that Billy disappeared. Mom was terribly upset, and Veronica decided: everything was to blame for the fact that she too often made this song sound. And she put the record, and hesitantly strummed her melody on the piano in the living room.

Then, when my mother was already in the clinic, Veronika often went to her room after traveling to her, put on headphones and listened to this song. Sad, high voices were a bit like mom's. She did not really understand the words, but for some reason they seemed to her correct.

When Leon left her, she again began to stage this song. She listened at night, instead of sleeping, imagined that the song was written specifically about her feelings. What you need only to explain is Leon, and he will become her again.

Even the number of green Volvo, on which they went to the clinic every Sunday, remained in memory. "KBH278". And also the smell that reigned in the old building, the number of steps from the entrance to my mother's room and how many shadow squares the grate cast on the stone floor when the sun shone through the window. Veronica could recall all this in a split second.

Other things - how the German verbs bow, what symbol means mercury, or in which year Charles the Twelfth was shot in the head with a brass button - on the contrary, they were completely forgotten, although she had once conceived them conscientiously. This is probably proof that the brain lives its own life and does not allow itself to be controlled. Not even allowing himself.

Veronika only remembered Askedalen that he was located somewhere in the Northern Forest and that there used to be a coal mine. The roads leading to the valley have long been removed, all of them overgrown with spruce. Veronica had a very vague idea of how to get there.

For more than an hour, she rode at random and finally found a narrow, half-overgrown trail leading, as she hoped, in the right direction. Five hundred meters she trudged along it, and then it ended.

Veronica got out of the car, pulled out a pocket flashlight, which she carried in the glove compartment, along with disks and inspection reports. I tried to determine in which direction Askedalen and how far to him.

In some ways she was lucky, in some things she was not. The direction turned out to be right, but it took almost an hour - twice as long as she expected - to wade through the thorny thickets before being in the deciduous forest. By that time, the sweater was already wet through with sweat, and the sneakers looked like two lumps of clay: in the lowland, where the sun did not reach, the liquid mud was perfectly preserved in the ruts left by the timber trucks.

Wandering through the forest gave her enough time to think. So, the blond was in the village. He introduced himself as Isak and visited Sailor in a nursing home. His appearance in the therapeutic group of Veronica is hardly an accident.

Sailor's fragmentary tale seemed to confirm that Tommy Root had abducted Billy, wanting revenge on Uncle Harald. If Isak is Billy, then Root did not kill him, as everyone thought. Then what happened after the abduction and what did Sailor mean when he said the truth was up there? Why did Isak appear only now, why didn't he let himself know so much? And if dad and Matthias are right and he is not Billy, then who is he and what does he want?

Other questions were no worse. How, for example, is all this connected with night events and a flat stone on the grave? Or here's another interesting question: why did she drag herself into the forest all alone and what she hopes to find here?

At the edge of the hollow, tired Veronica squatted down and tried to get an idea of the surrounding area. The slope here was too steep for timber carriers, trees and bushes formed a canopy, which did not allow to look down. For the same reason, the other side was barely visible, but Veronica estimated that the hollow should be at least two hundred meters wide.

The plate "ATTENTION! THE DANGER OF A BUNNING! ", Sitting askew on a tree trunk, aroused an old memory. Something Uncle Harald said that no one was hunting in Askadalen, fearing that the dogs or the hunter would fall into some kind of pit left over from the mine.

Veronica held her breath for a minute, and then began to carefully descend. The ground was covered with a thick blanket of dead leaves of varying degrees of decay, making the legs slipping and it was difficult to calculate the step. Halfway Veronica slipped, drove a few meters in the back, but grabbed a branch of birch and was able to rise to her feet. The bottom of the hollow opened before her. A green carpet of moss and grass, undergrowth, trees felled by the wind, which could not stay in loose soil. Veronica distinguished several places where the earth sank.

Below was almost absolute silence. One could only hear the woodpecker knocking somewhere in the distance. Foliage overhead let light through, turning it into green twilight. Looking around, Veronica realized that she was approximately in the middle of a hollow. You have to decide which way to go.

If she were Tommy Root or Sailor - poachers who need a safe place for the camp - she would look for somewhere higher. Veronica obeyed intuition and moved north, up the hill.

The ground was soft, and at every step the foot sank into it a few centimeters. The bottom of the hollow resembled a lunar landscape, only green. Most of the pits were no deeper than a couple of meters and about three times as large in diameter. The soil at the bottom of these pits looked quite ordinary, but Veronica did not want to experiment, checking whether it failed or not, and carefully avoided all the pits on the way up.

Ten minutes later she came across the first evidence of human presence. A pile of scrap metal, half corroded by rust. Veronica distinguished between a wheel and a block, she realized that these were parts of a lifting device. Immediately, she almost tripped over an almost completely overgrown concrete base - apparently, the foundation of some structure from those times when the mine was still operating. Looking up, Veronica noticed a deepening - perhaps the remains of a road that once led down. Now everything was overgrown with a thick fir tree, and this meant that the road was abandoned many years ago, long before Root and Sailor got here.

Veronica continued to climb up the slope; even found something like a path. It was too narrow and poorly trodden - Veronika decided that it was not laid by people, but roe deer, and she was right: hoof prints were visible in a pool of liquid mud. No horseshoes, no human footprints. No bonfire, no chopping, no huts - nothing indicated that people had recently come here. Theoretically, Veronica could be the first person to climb into these places since Seylor and Root were here .

She passed a bunch of half-rotten beams, noticed an iron skeleton on the ground next to them - judging by the wheel, the trolleys. Then on the way stood vast dense thickets. The path led right through them, and Veronica thought to go around them, then to return to the path again, but still decided not to turn off. Passing under the branches, she squatted, tilted her head - and almost stepped straight into the shed, barely noticeable among the greenery. Probably, it was built even when they dug a mine, and then abandoned it, or the land around the building became so unreliable that people did not dare to drive a bulldozer here.

In general, the barn was still here, although nature was trying with might and main to finish it off. Here and there shoots stuck between the gray boards, the tin roof was covered with moss, the leaves and grass formed such a heavy blanket that the walls sank.

Veronica took a step forward and felt something round under her foot. Bowing her head, she saw an empty moonshine bottle, half gone to the ground. Around the corner was another bottle.

The rest of the door lay on the ground, the door gap gaping in black. Something yellow and white hung from the roof. Stepping closer, Veronica saw that it was a "breeze" made of the bones of some animal and fragments of a horn, which, having drilled holes in them, were strung on a long leather cord. Suppressing a fit of nausea, Veronica went to the doorway and looked into the darkness.

Chapter 38

Once, as a child, they played hide and seek, and she hid in the barn, in the milking parlor. The old door jammed and an hour passed before it was found and released. All this hour she wept sobbing hoarsely and pounded on the door so that her hands ached.

She played, Matthias and his three friends. Matthias always knew how to make friends better than she. Not surprising. He was open, friendly and loyal, in addition, he was well given sports and various ball games. These guys are popular with both sexes, at least in the middle and high schools. Sometimes - honestly, quite often - she envied him.

That day she was rescued by her brother and his friends. They released from the milking parlor and did not say what happened to mom and dad. Veronica remembered how Matthias comforted her when she woke up later in the night; she had nightmares: darkness, damp, cold. A year later, when Billy had grown up for hide and seek, his father hung a bolt on the door and began to use the milking parlor to store winter tires. But the smell remained in her memory. And will be there while she is alive. A musty, raw smell, almost like in this barn. A couple of times Veronica even reminded herself that she was not nine years old and she no longer needed to be saved or comforted by her older brother.

She searched the barn in five minutes. A rusty heater, a log of wood and several bottles of beer and moonshine were discovered there. On a shelf was a cardboard with empty sleeves. Nearby lay a box of old-old matches from those that did not go out in the wind. What could be here has long disappeared. Of course, Veronica did not know for sure whether Sailor spoke about this place. But judging by the disgusting "breeze" and empty sleeves, the barn was an abandoned hunting hut, and the bottles indicated this with obvious evidence. There are hardly any other hunting huts in Askedalen. Intuition told Veronica that this is the place. But Veronica has not yet found answers to her questions.

Therefore, she decided to get out of the thickets and continue climbing the hollow, which was becoming narrower. It was darker here, as the path climbed, the slopes closer and closer and became steeper; the rock was exposed a couple of times. A black porous stone, similar to ashes - apparently, he gave the name [6] to the valley.

A big hole in the ground made Veronica stop. At least ten meters in diameter, it occupied the entire remainder of the trail. In the middle of a green funnel a black pit gaped. Water splashed, and Veronica realized that the pit was going even lower, to one of the walls of the mine. What if there, below, one of the vertical shafts? In this case, the hole could be truly deep. Twenty meters or more, and probably filled with water.

In the thicket just a few meters from the dip, the neck of another broken beer bottle stuck out. Veronica's pulse jumped. If you hide something in such a hole, tonikto will not find anything, and the bottle testified that Root and Sailor had been here.

Veronica decided to check whether she would be able to consider something deep down, without going down into the pit itself. It turned out not to succeed. The ground looked completely reliable, and Veronica became bolder. She carefully lowered both legs, pressed; nothing. She took a more confident step and began to move very, very slowly down to the pit. The splash of water intensified, and soon Veronica felt a moist underground smell, slightly reminiscent of the smell of the subway.

Now she could clearly see the opposite wall of the pit. A firmly pressed ground from which haustoria-like roots of parasitic plants stuck out like hairy worms. Below them is black rock and darkness.

Now Veronica's steps have become even shorter, about ten centimeters; finally she got to the edge. She took out a flashlight, directed a ray of light down and bent down to examine the hole. Slowly, carefully ...

The hole was not so deep - the bottom was visible only three to four meters from the edge. At the bottom was a pile of earth, leaves and stones - probably the remnants of a collapsed canopy, and then also debris with rains caused. Around the heap one could see puddles, the surface of which was constantly rippling - dripping from the edges of the pit. Water went into the darkness. There was probably emptiness below.

Veronica directed the beam of the flashlight lower, trying to see something among the shadows. A cheap lantern gave a thin, faint light, which was only enough for a few meters, and then it dissolved in the dark. Having shone to the right, Veronica saw something right on the border of the light cone. Trying to keep the lantern motionless, she squinted to see better. A light stick sticked out of a pile of garbage. Veronica strained her eyesight and realized that this is not a wand. This is a bone.

True, upstairs, Sailor's voice creaked in her head.

The crack in the chest widened, letting in icy cold. Blood rushed from the head, Veronica staggered. The edge of the pit suddenly settled, and Veronica flew down, right into the cold darkness.

My love

I'm trying to contact you, yesterday - by home phone, I drive by car past your house. I know that I am breaking the rules, breaking our agreement. But I don't know where you are, and this is driving me crazy.

I do not want to believe that you are leaving me. Leaving now when I need you more than ever. That all your words, your whispers were a lie. Or then they were true for you - as for me? And you believed that we really could be "we"?

I hate you - and at the same time I love you. And now - even stronger than before. Strange, right?

Chapter 39

Waking up, Veronica found herself lying face down at the bottom of the pit. The face is wet, the head is cracking, the taste of earth in the mouth. She must have hit hard, but the leaves and ground softened the fall; to her relief, Veronica realized that her hands and feet were intact. Apart from a few scratches and a headache, the most severe damage was a broken eyebrow. Veronica pressed the back of her hand to her forehead to stop the bleeding; at the same time she tried to orient herself. The flashlight landed in a puddle and did not work at first, but Veronika shook it a couple of times, slapped it with her palm, and he turned on.

She shone around. The cavern — or rather, the cave into which it failed, turned out to be larger than she thought — seven meters in diameter; the heap on which Veronica was sitting was located almost in the middle. The walls went up only a few meters, but the edges of the hole were now further apart. The pit was no longer the right circle - it collapsed from the side where the ground sank. Lumps of earth and pebbles still rolled into a large puddle at the feet of Veronica.

She shone into the darkness on the right and quickly found what she was looking for. A pile with a white bone sticking out of it.

The puddle was shallow, and Veronica's sneakers got wet through and through, and she went to the heap, not paying attention to the water. A flashlight lit up a bone and garbage - in any case, Veronica hoped that it was garbage. A pair of thin horns, scraps of skin and tendons, hooves. The remains of roe deer - probably the animal fell into the pit for a long time. Tense muscles were released, and fear came: Veronica began to understand what trouble had landed. She was in an abandoned drift, more often in the forest, where people rarely go - if they go in general.

Veronica climbed the heap again. To the edge of the pit too high, do not reach. Veronica looked around, looking for what to get up. She managed to find only a couple of rotten wooden supports under a pile of stones against the wall, as well as a tin kettle, which had been corroded by rust. There was nothing else here. Nothing that could help get out.

The flashlight blinked a couple of times and went out. Panic boomed in her chest, rose to the throat. The scanty light that penetrated the hole illuminated only a couple of square meters at the bottom of the pit. The rest was black and cold, like an old milking parlor. And this time there was no one to save Veronica. No one will come for her.

Veronica felt her breathing become intermittent - a clear sign of a panic attack.

She soon returned to the cone of light falling from above. She sat down on a pile and bent her head to her knees, trying to prevent hyperventilation.

Take a breath
Exhale
Whoo
Breathe out

Damn it, why did she climb here, rush into the senseless pursuit of a ghost? So I got it. Caught a fallen ...

Her head was spinning, blood from a broken eyebrow made her squint her eyes. For a few seconds, it seemed to her that she was about to lose consciousness. Ruud's voice sounded in his head.

Yes, calm down, Veronica, you must calm down! This is just a random hindrance. It must be overcome.

The hammer in the chest began to pound quieter and weaker. The cave, the pit, this whole damn hollow is just a hindrance that must be overcome. Like Leon, Ruud himself and her agreement with the union. Random interference.

She managed to breathe deeply, intermittently. Then again. Panic gradually loosened her grip.

Veronica got up and tried to bring the flashlight back to life by tapping it. He immediately came to life. Veronica stepped over the puddle and again searched the cave, this time more thoroughly. The side where the remains of the roe deer lay was facing the slope, and the bottom was dry. Just a few meters behind a pile of leftover skins, horns and bones, there was a smooth rock wall; this could mean that the drift ends here. Therefore, they dug a recess here - maybe they wanted to store something, otherwise where is the teapot from. And if the drift ends here, then the move is going the other way. Veronica looked at the puddle. From about the middle of the puddle, it expanded, going to the wall with props squeezed into it.

Closing closer, Veronica saw that the supports had once held a vault that had now collapsed. Water easily seeped between the stones and went down. It took Veronica just a few minutes to clear a place and light up the opening. From that side, it smelled strongly of damp and dungeon. But the draft was encouraging: it means that somewhere on that end there is another hole. She moved a couple of stones and shone again in the opening. The space on the other side expanded, becoming a small adit. The light of the flashlight flickered in the water that flooded the floor.

Wooden supports, sandwiched between the stones, allowed to carefully expand the hole so that Veronica could crawl into it. She turned around, looked at the safe rug of light under the hole. I tried not to think about the dark milking parlor.

Clutching a flashlight in her teeth, Veronica began to squeeze through the hole. The clothes were saturated with ice water, my breath caught.

Getting to the other side was easier than she expected, and now Veronica was standing in the aisle, almost straightened. A water mirror covering the floor reflected light. Water flowed from the cave that remained behind Veronica, and hundreds of drops and streams flowed along uneven, shiny rock walls. Almost immediately, Veronica realized that the water mirror was not motionless. That it glides slightly, flows into the darkness in front of her.

Rusty bolts stuck here and there. Probably, here once rails stretched, which were removed when the mine closed. Veronica, crouching, moved forward, lighting her way with a flashlight. Water splashed around, ripples made the shiny surface break, refracting the light of the flashlight.

Every three meters came across rotten, almost black wooden poles, squeezed into the transverse crossbeams in the ceiling. Veronica tried not to hit the props. She forbade herself to think how many tons of land and rock above her head, and continued to stubbornly move forward.

Laz went a little downhill and bent to the left. Veronica was convinced of the first, just looking at the water on the floor, but the second was more of a sensation. What if the course stretches to the side of the hollow with which it descended? Surely this is just one of the many mines lying at the ore depth and tearing the entire hollow. This thought bothered her all the more, the more water flowed from the walls of the drift.

Fifteen meters later, a thin layer of water underfoot turned into a sluggishly flowing river, reaching Veronica's ankles. Veronica stopped. The passage continued to descend, obviously following the hollow; this meant that water would only arrive. Veronica felt a faint draft. Somewhere deep below, where the mountain let air through, there was a hole.

After another ten meters, the water reached Veronica already to her knees, forcing him to go slower. The murmur grew louder. Water rose to the hips, then to the buttocks. The cold almost burned, it was hard to move. When the water got to the waist, and the flow was still stronger, Veronica understood what this meant. Yes, for sure, that's the collapse.

The ceiling collapsed, and the course almost completely overwhelmed with two huge boulders weighing probably several tons. Veronica shone between them, felt how the draft had intensified, and saw that the tunnel was abruptly wrapping up. But there was no further way.

She swore loudly - mainly to drive away the panic. The teeth pounded, the muscles in the arms and legs began to twitch involuntarily. Veronica still shone on the boulders, mechanically watching her as the water seeping beneath them. She ran her hand along the surface of the stone. At about the level of the knees I groped a hole - it seems wide enough so that you can swim into it. In any case, from this side it was wide.

Veronica shuddered from the cold, feeling how small cramps turn into trembling. How long does she have before the inner cold breaks her? Fifteen minutes? Less if she plunges into ice water entirely. What if she gets stuck halfway? You do not have to be seven spans in your forehead to anticipate such an opportunity.

The first time Veronica seriously thought about whether to return. Try to collect more stones, fold a pyramid high enough to get out of the pit. Then Veronica remembered that, making her way into this passage, she had already collected the stones left after the collapse, and even if she could collect more than her aspirations, they still would not be enough. Her only chance - unless, of course, she wants to sit in the pit and call for help that the case is obviously worthless - is to dive into the gap between the boulders. Try to get on the other side and get out where the air flows into the mine.

A breath of wind, breaking through the blockage, brought with it a faint smell of the forest, forcing Veronica to make up her mind. She turned off the flashlight and put it in her jeans pocket. She took a deep breath twice, exhaled. She bent her knees and plunged into icy black water.

A stream dragged her toward the hole faster than she had expected. The water was so cold that something seemed to explode in my head. The hole turned out to be small; Veronica rummaged in front of her, grabbed the unevenness on one of the stones and began to squeeze forward. Her eyes were open, but this did not help at all. The darkness here, below, was thick, as in a milking parlor. Veronica closed her eyes and began to gropingly focus on the road with her fingers.

Again she grabbed the stone with her right hand, and this thoroughly propelled her forward. She kicked off, hit her knee so hard that she almost stopped. Again she felt the space in front of her, leading her fingers along the ledges of the stone. She managed to advance almost half a meter, and then ... Something that she was afraid of happened. Veronica was stuck, she could not escape, helping herself with only one hand. There was less oxygen in the lungs, it was burned by cold and a pounding heart.

She managed to bend, stretch out her other hand. What else can you run into? Under the fingers there is only a smooth surface, and the irregularities are too small to grasp. The lungs burned, lightning flashed on the retina. The left hand seemed to fail and barely moved. Very soon the same thing will happen to the right.

The body did not move a centimeter, although the water around Veronica flowed faster. Oxygen was running out, it seemed to her that her lungs would explode now. A whole firework shimmered on the retina, but then it gradually turned black, as if in a picture tube of an old TV. Last thought, five words throbbed in my head.

You

Can not

Die

HERE!

Anger gave her strength. Veronica extended her right arm as far forward as possible. He burned his fingers, his hand was ready to give up when Veronica felt the edge. Probably the other side of the manhole between the stones.

Her fingers were pinched, but Veronica forced them to unclench. Of the last forces, she rested her right elbow, dodging her whole body. Pressure increased, water seethed around his head, gurgled in his ears. The mouth was about to open to take a breath and let the mines into the light black water.

Veronica, continuing to wriggle, clenched her teeth so that it cracked in her jaw. Suddenly she freed herself, and she suffered like a cork in a stream of wastewater. She hit her head, then her knee. Holding your breath was no longer possible. Veronica filled her lungs - but not with water, but with cold, moist air. Air with a faint smell of the forest.

Chapter 40

As she expected, the hole was right behind the bend. A ten-centimeter hole opened from the collapse, and earth poured around. With her numb, stiff hands, Veronica began to scoop up scraps of roots and stones. Earth flew into the face, Veronica had to close her eyes. The body shook uncontrollably from the cold. Within a few minutes, the hole had grown so much that it was possible, with your feet resting on the wall of the tunnel, to climb out.

Sticking her head and hands out, Veronica grabbed the tufts overgrown with grass. She began to pull herself forward, centimeter by centimeter, until her whole body was in warm air. Trembling, she rolled onto her back and suddenly laughed. Veronica laughed so that tears flowed from her eyes, and she no longer knew what the body was shaking from — from laughter or from the cold. She probably looked like some kind of forest monster. On the troll, on the evil gnome, who, wet, dirty, bloodied, roar out of the ground with a roar.

The fit of laughter passed, but Veronica continued to tremble with the cold. With her stiff, stiff fingers, she managed to pull off a wet sweater, but this only gave temporary relief. The body required heat, and much more than the forested hollow could offer.

Veronica estimated the distance and realized that it was not so far from the thicket where the hut was discovered. So she moved there.

The wood in the logs was, of course, incredibly old, but they were under the roof, and the wind, blowing through the boards, helped them stay dry. Fortunately, the storm matches that Veronica found before were also not wet, and only a few minutes later with the help of a few twigs of the funnel she managed to light a fire in a small hearth. Thanks for the ability to survive in the forest again had Uncle Harald.

Having undressed to underpants and a bra, Veronica hung up her wet clothes near the hearth and sat down, holding her hands over the fire. She felt a painful tingling sensation and almost laughed again. Sensitivity returned to the hands and fingers.

Veronica read about this phenomenon when she studied at the therapist, but she never really experienced it. The euphoria of the survivor. The feeling was reminiscent of a cocaine parish, and for several minutes Veronica thought that she was immortal and that nothing in this world bothered her. But as the body temperature recovered, the previous state of mind was restored.

What is the result of this idiotic outing? The answer is simple: no. Of course, Veronica found a hut - presumably Sailor and Roth, but there were no traces of Billy in it. Nothing confirmed his death, nothing indicated that he remained alive, and that is precisely what Veronica hoped in her heart. And even if Sailor's dementia brains were able to produce a few intelligible phrases, his muttering was hardly worth believing. Summa summarum [7], Veronica did not come close to answering any of the questions that did not give her rest. Isak's identity also remained a mystery.

Veronica picked out small pebbles from the soles of the sneakers and angrily threw them at the bramble, which grew near the barn. These pebbles crammed into the drift. Small, black, they crumbled in the fingers. Slag, coal of poor quality - these used to be crushed into gravel for sports fields and burning paths almost all over Skane or simply dumped somewhere in heaps. Veronica threw another pebble. Something tinkled metallic in the bramble.

Veronica looked in surprise towards the window, put on her wet sneakers, went out and threw another pebble into the dense bush. Something tinkled again, louder this time. There was something there - something that hid the thorny bush. Veronica returned to the barn, pulled on her pants and sweater, which had not yet completely dried out, but at least warm, and climbed into the bramble.

She moved cautiously, and yet a few thorns immediately dug into her legs. Other branches scratched her hands, and Veronica howled in pain.

She managed to take in a lot of stings, before one of her legs hard hit something. It immediately became clear that this was some kind of large subject covered with a dirty camouflage net.

Veronica tore the network, feeling the excitement grow. On the concrete base stood an iron caisson, a little larger than a washing machine. A large handle and two iron loops were visible on the upper bar. Caisson must have been used to store dynamite; it was large enough to accommodate an adult in a bent position. A small child would fit in it for sure.

The forging hammer pounding in his chest almost hurt; Before taking up the lid, Veronica forced herself to stand for a couple of seconds, her hands on her knees to suppress nausea. Standing like this, she noticed on the ground next to the concrete base the wreckage of a large castle, which obviously once hung in the hinges on the lid. Veronica raised the glands. The lock bracket was obliquely cut off - most likely by bolt cutters. The oblique slice, like the entire castle, thoroughly rusted. The castle must have lain here for many years.

Veronica sat up, took a deep breath and tried to lift the lid. Heavy, ten centimeters thick, she leaned on the second attempt and turned on dry creaking loops.

Caisson was almost empty, and Veronica exhaled. Inside, it was lined with boards. A shelf stretched along one wall - on it stood a spray can of weapon oil.

Clear. So, it was here that Root and Sailor kept their poaching rifles. Silenced rifles for which they did not have licenses and which they did not dare to keep at home.

At the bottom of the caisson, something gleamed. A brass sleeve stuck between the floorboards. Veronica hung over the edge, reached out and unscrewed the sleeve, and she inadvertently managed to pull out several boards.

Under them was opened space. Veronica examined a dark quadrangle and bent a little more. Her legs dangled in the air, and at some point she almost crawled right into the caisson, nose forward. Having regained balance, she tore some more boards and reached for an incomprehensible object. Green tin box, with a book the size of. Veronica pulled her to her and crawled out of the caisson.

The box was light; turning it around, Veronica found that she was unlocked and opened the lid. It's empty. The disappointment was so great that at first Veronica wanted to throw the find into the nearest bushes. But suddenly she noticed that something was sticking to the seam at the bottom of the casket. Some kind of white piece of paper. Veronica carefully pulled it out. The paper was folded in a triangular pocket; trying to tear it, Veronica realized: there is something inside. Something very thin, light, barely visible, something that instantly opened a crack in Veronika's chest, into which ice water poured.

Three short light hairs.

Chapter 41

When she returned to the port, where she left the car, it was already about seven in the evening. Clothes and shoes did not dry out and stank of mine water, but Veronica was warmed by the thought that she had got out of the crevice alive, and even wandering through the forest made blood run faster through the veins.

She held the box so as not to smear possible fingerprints. Lost in thought, Veronica did not notice the second car until she was right in front of her. A green pickup truck with the Aronson farm logo.

The driver stood leaning against the hood of her car. Aviator glasses, a green baseball cap, dark work pants. Flannel shirt with rolled up sleeves.

The man pressed a mobile phone to his ear; when Veronica left the forest, he turned to her. - Here she is. I'll call you back, "she heard his words.

It was Patrick, whom she met yesterday on the way to the farm. Patrick Brink, now she remembered. The son of one of the foremen Uncle Harald and cousin Cecilia.

The memory that she drove into the depths of her memory yesterday bubbled to the surface. 1986, she is soon seventeen. Mom died three years ago, as many years ago ABBA broke up, and Matthias lives in Stockholm. They gathered at a home party, sitting in the living room. The light is off, the air is stale from tension, the sound of my player sounds Take my breath away. Someone has her tongue in her mouth, the taste of tobacco and beer. A hand climbs under a sweater, then unfastens her pants on it. Veronica quickly drove away the memory.

Patrick Brink in those days belonged to the company "cool." Guys with a driver's license, whose life success came just in age between sixteen and twenty. Since then, Patrick has added ten pounds - it seems, mainly muscles, and youthful tendrils gave way to a well-groomed beard, but otherwise he has changed little. Self-confidence did not go away, and the weathered face looked, perhaps, even attractive. It seems that he belonged to that small category of people who, over the years, become more fit and attractive. Patrick took off his glasses and smiled broadly.

"What are you getting into, Vera?"

She caught her reflection in one of the car windows and realized that the question was, to put it mildly, justified. Clothes stained with ash, blood and earth. Face in black drips, hair hanging icicles.

"I fell," she said.

- Where? And what the hell are you doing here?

Veronica shrugged. She did not answer the first question and immediately went on to the second.

- I was looking for an old house, I was taken there as a child. But got lost.

Patrick looked as if he didn't believe her or simply thought he wasn't particularly smart.

"And how did you find it?" House?

- Mgm. - Veronica was tired of this conversation, she turned to the driver's door and began to rummage in her jeans pocket for keys.

- What is it? - Patrick nodded to the box.

"Yes, I found something."

- In the house?

Finding the key, she unlocked the car and quickly put the box on the floor by the passenger seat. When she turned around, Patrick was already standing on the other side of the open door ... perhaps too close. Veronica saw such a smile before - with other men. And the same gleam in the eyes.

"Everyone is looking for you, Vera." People are worried.

"You mean, my uncle." Did you call him now?

Patrick cast an expression on his face that did not confirm or refute her words. Then he smiled again.

- How long have you been working for him? - Veronika asked - mainly to wipe this smirk off his face.

- From the age of fifteen. With a break for the army and agricultural university. Harald convinced me to study further. Paid for maintenance and for training, was my mentor. And when my father retired, I became the foreman. But you all know this, of course.

Both his words and his tone provoked her. It's as if Patrick Brink is a person of unheard-of importance and talk about him reaches Veronica, who lives six hundred kilometers from here. Yes, she didn't remember him at all for many years.

"And so do you obey his orders?" What are you doing? She mechanically mirrored his tone. It worked better than she expected.

"I'm Harald's foreman, not an errand boy." Aronson pharming cannot do without me.

- Yah? Interestingly, Uncle Harald thinks so too?

Patrick moved even closer. There was a car door between them, but his presence felt like an obsession. Patrick glanced over Veronica, then looked up.

- And you're still the same. - The self-confident tone is back. "She's just as pretty, just a little more fit." More experienced. Remember - then, in the living room at Yucca? ..

Veronica surged into the temptation to tear the door toward her, and then push it back, so as to hit Patrick in the chest. Grab his hair while he gasps for air and poke a smug grin from his face. But she knew that she should not think about this, the lanky Bengt was right: such an attack of anger would not lead to anything good. Therefore, Veronica simply shrugged, slipped into the driver's seat and started the car.

"All I remember is that you had a small cock," she said, and slammed the door right in front of him.

Fatigue overtook her on her way home, and Veronica lowered the window so that the breeze would not let her doze off. The body paid for tension and adrenaline. Veronica understood that she had to resist, and yet thoughts began to mix, and consciousness filled with fog of the same indefinite hue as twilight outside the window.

The eyelids went down, the head went down, and although Veronica somehow understood what was going on, she could not resist it. The car went along the strip in zigzags, touched the left shoulder. Under the tire, gravel cracked warningly. But Veronica's head sounded "Take my breath away." Mom died, Billy disappeared, and Mattias threw her alone ... The car crossed the road again, it was carried to the right side of the road. Veronica's eyes closed, but in some surprising way she noticed everything that was happening to her. Veronica understood that she was about to leave for the ditch, and prepared for the accident, not taking anything to prevent it.

Something blinked right in front of her. Two brilliant points reflected the headlights. Someone's eyes gazed steadily at a car flying across the road.

The ability to respond instantly came to life. The foot pressed into the brake pedal so that the joints cracked, and Veronica at the last second managed to keep the car on the road. The brakes screeched, the tires creaked, the asphalt hissed. A short blow on the steering wheel - and then everything became quiet and calm.

Veronica sat in the car for some time - her heart was racing somewhere, her hands were trembling. The sickening smell of rubber and hot asphalt penetrated the open window. Veronica swallowed hard, pushed the door open. I got out to see what kind of beast she had moved. Three wind farms loomed in the field to the right of the car against the sky. Blinked her red eyes. Under a weak evening breeze, the blades moved slowly. They published a dull throbbing roar.

Stomach cramped. Veronica leaned on the hood, rounded the wing and prepared for the worst. She had seen encounters with wild animals before. I remembered how Uncle Harald grumbled at the weaklings who did not have the courage to finish off a wounded beast and abandon him, while he lay and screamed in mortal anguish. She knew how such screams sound. Appealing, full of horror - almost human.

But, circling the car, she heard only crickets and thuds - these were the hearts of giant windmills. Both headlights were intact; no blood, no wool, no dents on the bumper. There was no blood on the asphalt near the car. On her cotton legs, Veronica stepped to the side, and she vomited in a roadside ditch.

Chapter 42

When she drove into the yard, it began to get dark. Light was on in the house, and two more cars were standing on the headland next to his father's. One was Matthias, the other was a large, brilliant Land Rover. After a brief hesitation, Veronica decided not to take the tin box with her.

Carefully opening the door, she heard voices - all familiar. In addition to dad, here were Matthias, Cecilia and their three daughters. And also Uncle Harald and his wife Tess.

Veronica sneaked into the house, ran into the laundry room and washed off the most terrible drips of dirt and blood over the drain. Tied her hair in a ponytail on the top of her head. A pile of old clothes was found in a distant closet. Her own jogging pants, Matthias' old sweater ... Her sweater was several sizes large, but she hid a scar on her forearm. Veronica changed clothes, looked at her reflection in the window and gathered her courage to go out to the others.

Everyone was delighted with her, although she was late. Matthias and the girls were sincere, but Cecilia's joy was as simulated as her own.

Tess and Uncle Harald brought with them a son, Timothy. The last time Veronica saw him as a baby, and now he was five or six years old. Shy, he strove to hide under his dad's lap, to bury his face in his neck. Uncle Harald held him carefully, like a chick. His face glowed with pride, and although the dark-haired boy looked very much like his Thai mother, Veronica involuntarily thought of Billy. Glancing at her father, she knew from his glance that she was not alone. She was particularly reminded of by her brother when Tess called the boy Timmy.

Uncle Harald was like himself the same, only a little gray and flabby. Grandfathers sharp nose and thick eyebrows have not disappeared. The eyes have not changed. They look hard, carefully. But as soon as he looks at Timothy, the expression on his eyes changes, becomes softer, and Uncle Harald seems to be turning into another person.

"Say hello to your cousin Vera," he said, and winked at Veronica over the boy's head. "She had an interesting day today." She fluttered all over the district. Even, it seems, she glanced underground.

At the table, Veronica tried to catch Matthias's eye. However, the brother was completely absorbed in the role of a good husband, father and son.

Veronica studied Matthias, trying to understand what was going on between him and Cecilia. Just pretend for kids? In this case - pretend not bad. Matthias even took his wife by the hand - a gesture that surprised Veronica no less than Uncle Harald as a proud father. But most of all, she was struck by how pleasant the family dinner came out. Everyone spoke to everyone at the same time, filling the room, quiet at another time, with words and laughter. Even dad, who scurried between the dining room and the kitchen and brought either another bottle of wine, then new portions of food, looked a little happier and smiled restrainedly when everyone praised his cooking with enthusiasm. Even Uncle Harald's on-duty American stories didn't bore her now. Maybe wine played a role, but for a second Veronica thought that everything was as it should be. Almost ok. However, then she thought about the box left in the car. About a piece of paper with blond hair inside.

Timothy cheered up and ventured to sit on her lap while she read him a tale from a laced Disney book taken from a shelf. His chubby little hands were sticky with sweets, which his mother continued to palm off on him, although he had already eaten a double serving of dessert. He lowered Veronica's head to his chest; she could not resist and sniffed his crown. She inhaled a pleasant smell, which happens only in young children, and the ice in her chest began to crack and rumble again. The boy pulled out a sticky finger and poked at the picture. The animal with red fur and a sly smile.

"A fox," said the boy. - Dad shoots foxes. You too?

Uncle Harald turned to them, stroked his son on the head.

"Well, of course, Tim." All hunters shoot foxes as soon as they are seen.

- Why?

"Because there is only one hunter in the forest." - Uncle Harald winked slightly at Veronica over a glass of cognac to show: he was joking. But Veronica for some reason doubted this.

When it was time for the guests to leave, she went out with the others to the cars. The time was approaching eleven, the kids fell asleep, and they had to be carried in their arms. Veronica herself drank three cups of coffee and was now in that strange state when her body was already exhausted and her brain was awake.

It was only on Veronica Street that they finally managed to talk face to face with Matthias.

"I want to show you something," she whispered. - Found in the forest. I think this thing has to do with Billy.

- What exactly? - What a tense voice.

Veronica did not have time to answer - Uncle Harald came up from somewhere.

"How wonderful that you came." "It seems he really thought so." "Good when the whole family is assembled."

Veronica nodded silently, undecided with the answer.

"You can't live long without a family." What do you say, Matthias?

He slammed Mattias on the back, and Veronica noticed that her brother was embarrassed by this.

"Have you even talked to Ebbe?" There is nothing complicated. He only needs to sign, and we will arrange the rest.

- What to sign? Veronika asked quickly.

Harald and Matthias were silent for a few seconds. None of them seemed to want to answer her question.

- What exactly is dad supposed to sign? - repeated Veronica.

Before any of the men could speak, Tess honked out of the car.

"It's time to go," said Uncle Harald. "I was glad to see you, Vera." I hope we part for a while. He turned to Matthias and slapped him on the back again. - Call you tomorrow. And do not forget to talk with your father.

- What are you talking about? Veronika asked when they waved to Uncle Harald.

- He wants to build some windmills. Twice as high as today. Replace the old ones. - Matthias pointed into the darkness behind the house. - Dad must give consent to the construction.

- But why? Windmills obscure the view from that side of the house. They will be heard in the garden.

Matthias shrugged.

"It's a pity, but you will have to come to terms with this when you arrive at the weekend in about five years."

He said this not in a hostile way - simply stating, albeit perhaps in a slightly drunk voice. Nevertheless, Veronica upset his words.

"Matthias, are you coming?" Cecilia called out of the car. - I have to go. - Brother, it seems, regretted what was said when he realized that he had gone too far. - Call at the station tomorrow at about nine - we'll talk.

Veronica nodded. She stood looking after the jeep and wondering if she should pack up and get into her own car, as she was going to leave everything behind. Noona quickly sent these thoughts away. We need to show the box to Matthias - maybe he will be able to put together the elements of the puzzle. Veronica leisurely smoked.

Somewhere far in the dark a lonely nightingale sang.

Chapter 43

Veronica woke up because she was cold. The window was ajar and damp night penetrated the bedroom. I had to get out of bed and close the window. The body ached as if she had been beaten. The nails and knuckles were still black with coal dust, a deep cut over the eye disgustingly nagging. Veronica slept soundly, without dreams, but still did not feel rested.

The garden outside the window was almost motionless, only branches of trees swaying quietly under a gentle breeze. South wind. No signs of autumn, although August is drawing to a close.

When she went down to the kitchen, dad had already prepared her breakfast. Bacon, scrambled eggs, toasts. Even freshly squeezed orange juice. Veronica wanted to talk about the man she saw in the rose garden last night. Ask father why he didn't open when she knocked on the cabinet door, find out what makes him lock all the locks.

Find out what he and Sailor discussed when they drank beer at a pizzeria together. But dad, after yesterday's dinner, was in a good mood. He talked about grandchildren, smiled, stroked her head. And Veronica decided that the questioning could wait. First she will talk with Matthias.

"Will you stay for the weekend?" - asked the father - it seems, he decided that she had a vacation, although she did not say anything like that. - On Saturday in the park there will be a walk. I was not going to go, but you are here, and ...

Veronica diplomatically promised neither to stay nor to leave. She hastened to leave, so as not to see her father upset.

The local police station smelled of bureaucracy and detergent. Veronica hadn't come here before, so she had nothing to compare her current impressions with, but the reception room, where Matthias was waiting for her, looked like she imagined.

The walls in his brother's office were covered with pennants, tables framed with stripes and other police souvenirs from around the world. I wonder where they came from - inherited from his predecessor or did he really visit all these police institutions? Greater Manchester Police, Miami Dade Police Station, Rhineland-Palatinate Police. There was a pot-bellied monitor on the table, a police walkie-talkie from time to time popped and spewed out fragments of phrases, which they could not make out without effort.

Veronica went straight to the point and talked about the case in the rose garden. About a meeting with Aunt Berit, Lydia and her father, and then about her visit to Sailor in a nursing home. In a hurry to finish, until Matthias interrupted her with a question or doubted her words, she talked about the barn and the tin box she had found in the hidden caisson.

Veronica kept silent about her fall into the mine, as well as about the fact that Uncle Harald seemed to have sent Patrick to look after her. But Matthias heard enough. He put on rubber gloves, turned the casket this way and that, picked up a piece of paper with tweezers and examined the hairs under the magnifying glass. Veronica smiled - his brother was like a detective of old films.

"A corner," he muttered, "either to her or to himself."

- I'm sorry, what?

- Paper. The corner of the envelope.

- Yeah. - Veronica leaned forward, looking at a piece of paper, which his brother carefully held between his fingers. I saw that he was not mistaken. It is strange that she herself did not notice this. "What do you think this can mean?"

"We don't know for sure whose hair it is — Billy or not." - Mattias carefully put down a piece of paper. "We need to send them for analysis." Before we find out ...

- And if you skip this link? She interrupted. "Assuming Billy's hair?"

Matthias shrugged. He did not look as interested as she expected.

"Well, assuming it's really Billy's hair ..." Brother leaned back in his chair. "The police thought Root had abducted Billy to blackmail Uncle Harald." Then in the envelope from which this corner could be a letter with threats.

- And if there was no letter?

- As far as we know, he was not there. Maybe Root cut off Billy's lock of hair and put it in an envelope. Wrote a ransom letter. But for some reason he never sent it. Maybe things went awry, Billy died, and Root got rid of the letter. There was only a corner that accidentally got stuck in the box.

"Or it was different." - Veronica pulled out a photobot, smoothed it on the table in front of her brother. I saw his mouth tighten. - Someone similar to this image was visiting Sailor in Eckhagen. He introduced himself as Isak, told the nurses that he was the nephew of the old man. They remembered him well. And when I showed the photo to Sailor, it became clear that he recognized him.

Matthias glanced at the leaf, then at her. An interest finally appeared in the look. He was about to say something when a door was suddenly knocked on and a woman of about thirty looked into the office. According to the expression that appeared on her face when she saw that Matthias was not alone, Veronica immediately realized who it was.

- Oh, sorry. I didn't know that you had a visitor. - The stranger stood in the doorway. Beautiful, dark eyes, skin almost the same bronze hue as Leon.

- This is my sister. - It seems that Matthias felt uncomfortable.

- A. Hello! - The woman smiled, but did not introduce herself. Matthias was silent too.

- Something urgent?

- No, it suffers. Nice to meet you. - The woman nodded to Veronica and closed the door behind herself.

Matthias avoided her gaze, and Veronica did not know what to do with the tension in the office. Matthias, apparently, too - and therefore he resolutely rose from his chair.

"Come on, I'll show you something."

Following her brother, she went down the stairs, passed a row of closets, two changing rooms and an open door that led to a small gym. Having passed the corridor, they found themselves at the armored door with the "Archive" sign.

The room - a square box with no windows - was spacious, but Veronica still remembered the old milking parlor. She closed her eyes, swallowed.

Smells of ink, dust and paper floated in dry air. The middle passage led to racks filled with folders, newspaper binders and cardboard boxes. Veronica read the years on the shelves: 1998, 1995, 1993. Matthias went to the very corner, up to 1983, and stopped. He pointed to a rack near the wall. A row of blue folders, all with the same number.

"This is Billy's business." Nineteen full folders that Monson left behind. I read them all ten times, thoroughly studied each interrogation protocol, each autopsy report, each note. - He ran a finger along the cardboard roots. - No matter what people say, Monson did everything he could. He continued to scour the area in search of Billy even after the prosecutor closed the case. I personally received and checked information from the population, regardless of how plausible or fantastic the messages were. He hoped that Root would be returning home.

- Visited? - Veronica guessed the answer even before Matthias shook his head.

- The last sign of life is an empty postcard, postmark - Rotterdam, addressed to Nille Root. She arrived about a month after the disappearance of Roth. Sven Postman handed her over to the police. I think Monson showed her to Nille. A postcard is here somewhere. I saw her myself.

He pointed to the folders.

- On a postcard, a cargo ship. Apparently, Root went to sea. Monson phoned sailor churches and hotels in Rotterdam and other port cities. Root was still their only suspect, the only one who had a motive, so I understand why Monson did not want to give up. He hoped to find out where Root was found, hoped that he would find more evidence, and, of course, wanted to find out where our Billy's body was. But he did not achieve anything.

- What about the car? Roth's old Amazon? What with her?

- They didn't find the car either.

"What about Monson?"

- He returned to Ostergotland. In Mjolby, I heard. What's the difference. Most blamed him on Roth's release. In my opinion, unfair. I'm not sure I would do better. - Matthias shrugged barely.

"Is he still alive?"

- I think yes. Someone said that he was sick. Stomach cancer or something like that. Do you remember Monson?

Veronica nodded.

- Always so troublesome, and spoke funny. Estonian dialect, con words. I remember that he had kind eyes.

And I lied to him about the fact that we returned home together, thought Veronica. So you don't get stuck in history. Because at that time we were - and the rest of the world is against us.

"And what would you say about all this?"

Matthias turned to her.

"You were in Billy's room after that summer?" Or in my mother's, for that matter?

Veronica shook her head.

- They are locked.

- Do you know why?

- Not. - Veronica had the answer, but she preferred to pretend to be a simpleton.

- I tried to persuade dad to move to the village. Settle in a house in several apartments, closer to the grandchildren. Uncle Harald offers to buy Bakkagorden for a good price.

- But?

- Dad refuses to move. She doesn't even want to hear. And refuses to sign a building permit for Uncle Harald. He paused, as if pondering something. - What I want to say: a person should be able to let go of his past. Otherwise, he will get stuck in it like that.

They returned to the office. Matthias went into the kitchen, brought two chipped coffee mugs. The area was almost quiet, only the radio sometimes grumbled, and from somewhere in the deep corridor came a click of the keyboard.

"I'll send my hair to the lab today," Matthias said as they drank a sip of coffee. "But even if it's Billy's hair, we're unlikely to get far."

Veronica nodded - she had already figured out such an option.

"Then I'll talk to the nursing home, I'll ask the manager to call if this Isak shows up again," continued Matthias. - And as for the pope and that person whom, in your words, you pursued in the garden ...

- What do you mean by your words? There was definitely someone there!

Matthias put down his mug and raised his hands.

- Sorry, I put it wrong. If I understand correctly, you have not seen a person. Just like in Stockholm.

"I'm sure someone was there!" - Veronica tried to restrain herself, not to let anger win. What a pity it is so easy to get angry with Matthias.

"Could it be a roe deer?"

"Roe deer that lowered the gate valve?"

- I'm just asking. - Matthias raised his hands again.

They stared at each other angrily for a few seconds, then Matthias capitulated.

- At the beginning of summer, someone thoroughly rummaged in distant, solitary estates. I will make sure that the night patrol drove past dad from time to time.

"Good," Veronica said, and added more gently: "Thank you."

They were silent for a moment.

- Will you stay for the weekend? There will be a walk in the park. Uncle Harald supplies the whole village with refreshments and drinks. Live music promised.

- What is it with him? Why did he suddenly become generous?

Matthias grinned.

- The story with the new windmills diminished his popularity. So he is trying to buy a neighborhood location.

- Clear. - Veronica carefully answered the smile of her brother. I felt the tension still reigning in the study abate. "But how ..." she nodded at the door. "Your family therapy?"

His brother's smile turned into a grimace.

"Not particularly good, to be honest." I try very hard, but everything is so complicated ... Cecilia and I have known each other since school. We have a common house, common children. You can't leave everything.

Veronica thought about Leon and almost began to tell Matthias about him - after all, now the trust between her and her brother was restored. But instead she asked:

- Do you love her? "And only then I realized how ambiguous the question was."

- Love is different. - Brother shrugged.

Veronica nodded, scratched the scar on her hand.

"Does Uncle Harald know about your problems?"

Matthias shook his head.

- I only told dad. Cecilia and I try to sweep everything under the carpet. For the sake of girls.

And also because you knew Uncle Harald's reaction in advance, thought Veronica. He will begin to press, to demand that you stay with Cecilia, acted as he considers correct. And it will be very difficult for you to resist him. Because you are a good boy. Son of Ebbe and Magdalena.

She decided to change the subject, take a moment of sincerity and ask a question that had remained in the background for so long.

"How do you think ... mom loved us?" Well, that's understandable,
"she said quickly, anticipating possible protests," that there is
nothing worse than losing a child. " But she still had us. Why was
she missing us?

Why?

A word hung in the air between them, and for a while they drank
coffee in silence.

"Do you feel guilty of something?" Asked Matthias, and she
cringed. "Billy knew how to be a true punishment." As then, for
example, when he nayabednichal mom about the nest. And mother
always treated him differently, as if he were some kind of ...

- Special.

- Exactly. As if there were other rules for him. - Matthias smiled
awkwardly, and Veronica felt a little better.

- Billy called their mom and dad, remember? And we said - mom,
dad.

"I remember how." - Matthias grinned. "We started calling them
mom and dad after ..." He paused, turned away.

Veronica took a deep breath. So what, that in the chest ice.

"I was mad at Billy that night." Thought he hid somewhere and fell
asleep. Mom will get upset, and you will get into it because you
came home late. What will happen, then with a nest. I searched
everywhere, both in the barn and in the barn, called in different ways
- both aloud and to myself. I still dream about it. That I seek him and
do not find.

Veronica stopped, afraid that she had spoken too much. But
nothing could be understood from Mattias's face.

- And you? She asked. - What do you feel?

She remembered the folders in the archive. Matthias read them
more than once, page after page, trying to find something that no one
had paid attention to him. Something that would fix everything,
although he guessed that it was impossible. Something that will
explain the inexplicable. Is she herself like that? Is this really the
whole point? She wanted to say no, to convince herself that she was
different.

"Sometimes ..." Mattias began. Was silent for a while. Rubbed his
neck. - Sometimes it seems to me that the summer goes on. That we
are somehow still there. Dad, you and me. The whole village ...

Brother interrupted the phone. Suddenly a sharp bell made him
startle. The softened gaze was again softened. - Hello? Yes hi...

Veronica understood from his voice: Cecilia was calling. Consequently, the conversation is over.

Chapter 44

Veronica faintly remembered Roth's farm. Several dilapidated buildings somewhere on the edge of the Northern Forest, gray roofs that could be seen from the country side. She rode back and forth several times, it seemed, where necessary, but she saw neither the congress nor the roofs. On the field next to the road stood a huge green tractor with a disk plow. The tractor driver just jumped to the ground to fit the hydraulic hoses. Veronica stopped the car and went to a stranger - a man of about thirty.

"You don't know where Roth's estate is?" She asked.

The man smiled and shook his head.

- Only speak English [8].

Veronica tried again, in English, but the tractor driver spoke with such an accent that it was not easy to understand. At the end, he pointed to the opposite edge of the field, where, near the forest edge, a compartment of trees was visible.

- Maybe there [9].

Veronica went through a field bristling with bare stems. It turned out to be wider than she expected, seven hundred to eight hundred meters, no less, and her battered body expressed discontent. The breeze died down, the sun was high, so when Veronica entered the shade under the trees, she was already pretty sweaty.

Despite the words of the tractor driver, no buildings were found in the grove. There was only a clearing, similar to an overgrown headland. Beyond it, to the very edge of the forest, a bristly field stretched again. There were no buildings in sight.

Veronica swore. But soon, when her eyes got used to the twilight under the trees, she realized that the tractor driver was still right. The land in the clearing was so trodden that the grass could not break through it. In a couple of places, the remains of masonry were visible, and on the very edge a heap of broken brick stood. Expanding the circle of searches and moving the nettle toe sneakers, Veronika found several pieces of iron, boards and fragments of tiles. Roth's compound was really here. But now it has disappeared. He was razed to the ground, almost uprooted.

She really did not like something in this dark meadow, and she finally understood what was happening. In silence. There was silence in the clearing. The birds did not sing, the leaves did not rustle. Only came from afar the hum of the tractor. Veronica could not say where this feeling came from, she was never superstitious, but she suddenly thought that something had happened at this place. Something that has not yet ended.

The tractor approached, but when Veronica turned and looked at the field, she found that the sound was coming from a large green "Land Rover," which was driving towards her right along the chopping stubble.

Veronica recognized the car and moved towards her. The car stopped near the grove, Uncle Harald got out and stretched slightly.

"You, I see, set off again in search of adventure."

"I'm looking for Roth's manor."

- I got what you mean. - Uncle Harald stepped towards her. "Why is there so much interest in Tommy Roth?"

Veronica ignored the question and pointed to the clearing behind them.

- What happened to the estate?

"The bank took her."

Uncle Harald took a pipe from his breast pocket, carefully filled it and lit it.

- Roth was very unimportant with the scores. The bank threatened to describe the property, and Roth needed the money. Therefore, he did what he did.

Uncle Harald fell silent and took a long drag. Sweet, strong smoke. Veronica saw a thousand times how his uncle smokes a pipe.

- What about the family?

- Left here a year later. They did not like them here from the very beginning, and after Billy ... - He did not finish, but Veronica easily guessed the end of the phrase.

"But Nilla and the children have nothing to do with it?"

- Who knows what was known or not known to Nille Root. - Uncle Harald shrugged. "I heard that the social service in Malmö took her children from her." Maybe this is the answer to the question.

Uncle Harald puffed out his pipe again.

- Did you buy a manor from a bank?

He nodded.

"Fifty tunlands [10] of first-class arable land." The best in Skane.

- And the buildings?

"I told them to be torn down." - Uncle shrugged again. But Veronica caught the change in his voice.

- What, completely pimped?

- No, the estate could have been cleaned up if you wanted.

"Then why did you demolish everything?"

Uncle Harald took the pipe from his mouth, looked at Veronica. Deep set eyes darkened.

"For the sake of Magdalena."

He coughed, clearing his throat. It looked like his voice was about to change him, and Veronica thought: is it anger or sadness? Or maybe both.

"My father ... Your grandfather Assar - do you remember him?"

- Not really. I was only eight when he died. - Such a quick change of topic surprised her a little. - They did not communicate with mom - this is me, in any case, I remember well. And what?

"Assar has always been difficult." - Uncle Harald smiled wryly. - He was an old school, but not afraid of new ideas. Not afraid to take risks. When he realized that the war was not far off, he realized how much he needed to carry. Food, fuel, people. Therefore, he spent all his savings, mortgaged the estate and bought some old trucks and buses, and then supplied them with gas engines.

Uncle Harald gnawed the pipe, blew out more smoke.

- And when the war began, he was ready. He signed a contract with the defense industry and with neighboring communes. Worked day and night. Earned money spent on the purchase of real estate and arable land. He already understood that a business of this magnitude would end soon. We must look forward. Try new crops, new methods. Thanks to your grandfather, I decided to build wind farms, long before the others.

- But what about the rumors? - asked Veronica. - That somewhere near the end of the war, large reserves of the gas mixture were found in the defense depots, that the new cargo bodies were replaced with old, scratched ones? What did grandfather have to do with this and turned out to be the main suspect, but paid someone who went to prison instead of him?

As she expected, Uncle Harald's contented smile instantly disappeared.

- Gossip. The lies and slander of people who were jealous of their father. Wow, what nonsense they are talking about!

The tube went out. Uncle Harald pounded her on the heel of a rubber boot. Trampled ashes.

"You rarely go home, Vera, so I don't expect you to understand." But if you act like in America ... Constantly look forward. Do not get stuck in the past. Those who do not understand this ...

"Do you mean those who do not support your plans to turn the village into a megapark of wind farms?"

Uncle Harald let out a cross between a scornful snort and a laugh.

"Sometimes you look so much like a mother that you take a creep." Just wonder, just think that you know everything better than others. Always right. - Uncle Harald shook his head and put the receiver in his breast pocket. "The future always comes, Vera." Whether a person wants it or not. But the past never comes again.

He turned away, intending to return to the car.

"What if Tommy Root didn't kill Billy?" - blurted out Veronica. "What if everything was different and Billy is still alive?"

Uncle Harald stopped. Veronica was waiting for him to worry. He will ask what it is she carries. But he only snorted.

"Well, yes, I heard that you have your own theory." That you show everyone some pictures.

He stepped towards Veronica, bowed his head to one side and let go into the voice of gentleness, from which it became immediately harder to get angry at him.

"Vera, Billy won't be back." Tommy Root killed him and escaped punishment. And he took the life of your mother, my little sister. Unlike your father, I am not one of those who plant roses. I thought you and I were alike in this.

Something in her uncle's tone touched her. A note of frustration? Veronica did not know what to do with her.

"Your brother is lying somewhere in the forest," continued Uncle Harald. "All alone, in an anonymous grave, and not in a cemetery next to his mother." And Tommy Root sent him there. I hope he burns in hell for that.

He came closer, put a hand on her shoulder. Veronica's first impulse was to move aside, but the uncle's gesture seemed sincere, like the sadness in his eyes.

"However, all this belongs to the past." And we must look to the future. You, your father, I am the whole county. You see, Vera, what do I mean?

Chapter 45

When Veronica returned, the house was locked again, but dad, as always, left a spare key. The cart shed where he was putting the car was gaping empty - apparently, his father had gone to the village to shop. Veronica entered the office, called her answering machine - didn't Ruud leave a message.

There were three new messages. The first two are weak breathing, and then rattle: the caller hung up. For a moment Veronica hoped it was Leon; stupid thought! Why would Leon call her if he struggled to get an official ban on contact?

She turned on the third message, expecting a rattle to ring again. But with surprise I heard:

- This is Lars. From the group. I would like to speak with you as soon as possible. Call me. - A rough voice rumbled a few numbers and with a click fell into oblivion, without saying goodbye and without explaining what was the matter.

Lars is the man with the beard that Ruud forbade to come to therapy. What does he want from her and how did he get her number? Veronica once again listened to the message, but this did not add clarity. At the same time, she was sorting through the papers lying on her desk. The agreement on building consent was in the same place, still not signed.

Veronica pulled out the top drawer. In a small compartment for pens, paper clips and erasers, an old door key was discovered. She shook it in the palm of her hand, thinking what Matthias would say about the locked doors on the top floor. I looked out the window - whether there was a father's car on the site - and decided.

Billy's room, which had once been her room, was located to the right of the stairs. The key turned easily; Veronica darted in and closed the door behind her. The room smelled of carpet and Ajax. The roller blind is half-lowered, and the room rests in the darkness.

Above the bed hung a large photograph of Billy. The same, made in the studio, which was stored at home at Veronica. Veronica saw her in a newspaper article, albeit significantly enlarged. Billy laughed at the camera, showing milk teeth and dimples on the soft cheeks. Blue eyes shone. Veronica had to swallow hard to prevent the cold from spreading in her chest.

Next to the photograph was a drawing of Billy, who was apparently trying to portray a rabbit on it. On the bed, leaning against the blue and white wallpaper, were sitting soft toys in an even row.

Veronica carefully walked around the room. She began by opening a wardrobe, which turned out to be much smaller than she remembered. On the shelves were the little things of a little boy. Veronica thought: I wonder if Billy checked the lock on the door three times before lying down. She herself checked. A wooden gun was lined up against the wall between the bed and the bookcase. It seems that Billy received it for Christmas as a gift from Uncle Harald. Veronica thought that the younger brother also heard a lot of terrible tales and armed himself against nightmares. From this thought hurt in the chest.

On the top bookshelf were wooden toys. Tractor with a trailer - the wheels spin, the trailer is on a magnet. Nearby is a harrow, the teeth are made of an iron comb. Both toys are expertly carved and neatly painted. Veronica knew that dad made them in his workshop. Probably spent more than one hour to get them flawless.

Books lined up under the toys about Tot-those inherited by Billy from Veronica; next to it were seashells and flat pebbles, which the brother had probably brought from several of his trips to the sea. Sixty kilometers from the sea - less than an hour by car. And yet they did not go there often. From the sea, my mother became restless. Veronikasnova thought about that pebble on the grave. A pebble from the sea. I regretted not taking it with me.

On the third shelf houses from "Lego" flaunted. Difficult for the five-year plan - Matthias probably helped to build them. Next to the models was a blue portable player. There was a record on his turntable. Judging by a few specks of dust on black vinyl and the smell of detergent, dad cleaned here just a couple of days ago. Probably, bed linen changed. Veronica carefully ran her hand over the pillow. Pillowcases, duvet cover, freshly ironed sheet. They smell like washing powder.

In the middle of the desk was another house of Lego. Unfinished. A few details are scattered around - as if they were waiting for the owner of the room to return and attach them to the right places. Near the house there is a vase with a single white rose. Surely from the bush, under which dad cleaned up on Saturday when she arrived. Beautiful fresh rose. Veronica leaned over and sniffed a flower. Moved the parts, raised the house, put it in place. I switched to the player. Once upon a time, he also belonged to her, she received it as a gift for Christmas from mom and dad. When she later moved into Matthias's room, he already had a real stereo player, bought with the money that Matthias earned in the summer at the hardware store, so the portable player stayed here with Billy.

Veronica raised the lever. There was a click, and the record spun. After a couple of moments, she gained the required thirty-three revolutions per minute. Veronica lowered the needle to the vinyl, heard the rattle in the speakers. How well she remembered this tale - she recognized right away, from the narrator's voice. "The mouse and other inhabitants of the forest of Elki-na-Gorka."

She sat on the bed and began to listen to the story about the animals, wondering that she still remembers almost every remark by heart, although she had not heard this record since childhood. She and her mother were lying on this bed and together they listened to a fairy tale.

You are my mouse, Vera. My little mouse.

A crack in the chest opened, became a black hole. Veronica lay down, buried her head in the pillow. She smelled not only of laundry detergent, but of Billy and mom.

Veronica did not cry, having learned that her mother had died, she did not cry at the funeral, although everyone cried there, even Uncle Harald. But the smells of the pillow, the children's fairy tale on the scratched record and this sad room, which was quietly waiting for the little boy, broke some kind of barrier.

Veronica sobbed so that she was shaking all over. The narrator continued the story about the Elki-na-Gorka forest, and when Veronika cried and her tears gave way to a paralyzing weakness, the needle reached the last path. To the "Lullaby Mouse" - her favorite song.

She closed her eyes, listening to the familiar tune. For a moment she was five years old again. She had a terrible dream, she woke up scared. Mom is here. Lies nearby and whispers something in her ear. Makes the nightmare fade.

Go to sleep, baby, gray mouse. We cover the tail, dreams will come to visit us.

She felt mom's breath on her neck. The warmth of her body, the smell of her perfume. Veronica curled up, listening further.

Both owls and cats sleep, fall asleep, baby, and you.

She wanted to tell her mother that she did not interfere. What remains to be done as much as he wants. But the song was short, lasted only a minute, and now the pickup already reached the last line. To the word, behind which terrible dreams always crawled into the darkness again. Veronica closed her eyes, whispering words.

In the fox mink on the bed, even Fox went to bed [11].

When the song ended, mom softly kissed her on the cheek. The bed creaked, the floor quietly responded to easy steps. A breath of air - and she disappeared.

Chapter 46

If you go to bed in your children's bedroom, the bed will seem smaller than I remembered, and the walls and ceiling are as if approaching you. But the smells, the touch of a rough sheet on the skin, the sounds that give rise to an echo in the room do not change over time. Everything here is so familiar, so safe. And - giving rise to anxiety.

Maybe that's why she didn't want to come here. It is unbearable to feel that she is no longer at home here, that she will never be here again.

Veronica was woken up by a phone call. She heard her father's footsteps on the ground floor, then a quiet "hello."

Only a few seconds later she realized where she was. The player turned off, the needle and foot pressed into the holder. Veronica quickly whipped up the pillow, smoothed out the blanket and bedspread.

- Vera! - shouted from below the father. - Are you there?

The shame that she was exposed, that she had done something forbidden, burned her. Veronica cast a last look at the room, made sure that everything looked as before her arrival, and closed the door as quietly as possible.

- I'm coming! She shouted a little louder than required, and turned the key in the lock.

Veronica went down two steps and just wanted to put the key in her pocket when she ran into her father. They froze opposite each other - at such a short distance that both felt awkward.

- Is everything okay? - asked the father. "You're kind of shaken up."

Veronica held the key in her fist, and tried to hold her hand behind her back.

- Yes, I lay down for an hour. Is that me?

Veronica nodded to the hallway: she wanted to sneak out. But the father did not move and looked at her as if trying to understand whether she was lying or not.

"Phone," said Veronica. - Is that me?

- Someone from work. - Father slightly stepped back.

Veronica hurried down the stairs, feeling her father's gaze on her back. Father went to the second floor; Veronica thought she heard the handle on Billy's door turn. She darted into the office, pulled out a desk drawer and returned the key to its place, after which she picked up the telephone receiver lying on a stack of papers. It turned out to be Ruud.

- It's not easy to get through to you. Have you heard about mobile phones?

- Yeah. - Veronica tried to figure out where he got this number. Maybe she wrote it in some form when she was just starting to work at the Center? For example, in the column "Immediate Relatives." Probably it was.

- What are you doing in Skane? Asked Ruud.

- Nothing special. So, a little sortie. - Veronica scolded herself for the fact that her brains shaken like scrambled eggs did not come up with something better, but Ruud seemed satisfied with this explanation.

"I have good news," he began; the sound was as if he had brought the receiver closer to his mouth. - Bengt made a report. His verdict is that you can continue to work. And I managed to convince the personnel department of this. Come and I will tell more. Will you be back in Stockholm by noon tomorrow?

- Of course. Not a problem. - Veronica hung up, realizing that she should be happy. She kept her job, got the opportunity to see Isak again and at the same time satisfied that part of her inner self that required more grief. The grief of other people, not the one that Bakkagorden was full of. However, she didn't come.

Before her departure, dad prepared an early dinner. They ate an omelet in the kitchen, and Veronica felt that something had changed between them, but could not understand what it was. She should definitely deal with this before leaving here.

"I was at my mother's grave yesterday," she began. - Very beautiful. Roses ...

- Mm. - Father nodded, not ceasing to chew.

What else to say? Anything to soften it.

"How long would you be married now?" - These words escaped from her by themselves, but it seems to have worked. Father raised his eyes.

"The thirteenth of January." Thirty six years old.

"Well, yes ..." Veronica bit her lip: she did not call him on the last anniversary of her parental wedding and now came up with an excuse. But suddenly a smile appeared on his father's face.

- The night before it was snowing and a strong wind was blowing. We even doubted that we could even get to the church. Road cars could not cope. But your grandfather, mother's father, caught up with the tractors of all the neighbors here. - He shook his head.

- Are you cold? - Veronica seized on this topic.

- And how! I was fine in a tailcoat. And Magdalena put on her mother's wedding dress, thin silk, so she probably froze to the bone. Her hands were icy. But she never complained.

- And where did you celebrate?

"Your mom's parents." There were not many guests, mostly relatives. Wait a minute ... - Father got up, went into the office, and Veronica heard him looking for something.

- Here.

He laid a black and white photograph on the table. Veronica had seen wedding photos of her parents before, but this is the first time. In any case, she did not remember him.

It was a family photograph taken in the living room of my grandparents in Engsgarden. The newlyweds are standing in the center, and on the sides of them are the parents of the bride and groom. Around - vases with bouquets.

Grandfather Assar, strict, focused, stands a little behind mom. The similarity between him and Uncle Harald, on the far right, was noticeable even then. Those deep-set eyes, powerful eyebrows, a sharp nose. My grandmother looks more meek. She smiles tightly at the camera, her cheekbones high, like her mother. And Veronica.

Dad's parents are much more fun. The Nilsons are typical friendly farmers from Skane who grew up on goose and meringue cakes, and the contrast with the lanky, stiff, slightly arrogant Aronsons is striking.

Dad smiles broadly, there is so much happiness in his gaze that it seems to pour from a photograph. Veronica smiled involuntarily.

Mom also smiles, but there is something strange in her expression. Veronica did not immediately understand what was happening. In a small photograph of my mother's eyes were smaller than a pinhead. Veronica peered - and recognized this look. She saw him in the mirror and knew perfectly what he was talking about. Ah, how bad.

"She could choose anyone ..." muttered dad, and Veronica did not understand if he was talking to her or talking to himself. "But she chose me."

When she left, everything was almost as always. She hugged her father, kissed on the cheek. She promised to go leisurely and call when she gets home. The wind rose, the warm south wind, and the large blades of the giants waved her goodbye. Veronica left the plain behind.

The old car did not tolerate the heat well, and less than four hours later Veronika had to stop at a gas station to add water to the cooling system. Dad gave her a bag of food - carefully prepared sandwiches with cheese and ham - and a thermos of coffee, so she at the same time arranged for herself a short lunch break.

Veronica hoped that the trip would give her the opportunity to ponder the events of recent days. Understand your own thoughts about a man who calls himself Isak. Is that really Billy? Heading to her father, Veronica was almost convinced of this. Now confidence has diminished. The feeling that led her to Askedalen disappeared, but questions remained.

Veronica understood how lucky she was that she kept her job. She lacked the therapy of grief, she did not have the buzz. The best thing now is to focus on the group sessions and wait patiently for Isak, who may give her a few more guiding threads.

The strategy looked reasonable; Veronica finished her coffee and decided that the rest was over. Then she noticed at the base of the thermos a piece of adhesive tape with the inscription Property of the Nielson family. Familiar mother's handwriting with curls. The adhesive tape with the edge was a little behind, and Veronica wanted to tear it at all, but quickly changed her mind. Mom taught her old-fashioned calligraphy. She taught me to write in beautiful letters, completely unlike the ones that fill her notebook, absorbing human feelings. She thought again about Leon, about the words that she had written to him and which she now repented. She hoped these words would help, but they did the opposite.

Maybe that was what Tommy Root reasoned about when he sent his wife that postcard from Rotterdam? Matthias said there was no sender address on her. There was nothing at all - not even a request for forgiveness. But he abandoned his family. Did Tommy Root understand what she herself refused to recognize? What sometimes words do not help?

Veronica, ready to move on, put the thermos in her bag. Started the engine, sat for a while, thinking. In front of her was an Estonian plain. Flat fields, almost at home. Native land Christer Monson. Christer Monson with kind eyes and a funny manner of speaking.

Veronica turned off the engine. I wonder if there is a phone in a gas station at a gas station. She got out of the car and went to the diner.

Chapter 47

Christer Monson just poured the dough into the mold when he noticed that Bella was rushing to the door. The claws scratched the parquet, an impatient barking was heard, and a bell rang. Mondays, she and Bella spent alone at home. Malin and her friends went to a meeting of the book club, and instead of waiting for her in front of the TV, Christer baked cookies for coffee so that his wife had something to bring with her to the teacher's room the next day. He liked that she returned with an empty can and told how everyone praised his pastries. Muffin with rhubarb was his favorite, Monson baked it every third week.

Bella continued to bark. Monson hung his apron on a chair and stepped out into the hallway. Behind the frosted door glass loomed a vague figure.

"Quiet, Bella," he said, but the baby terrier, as always, did not obey, so Monson simply pushed the dog away with his foot and opened the door.

- Hello! - On the threshold stood a woman of about thirty with reddish hair. In the light of the light bulb above the porch, it seemed to him that this was one of Malin's colleagues. Bella kept barking; Monson wanted to say that Malin would not be there for several more hours, but suddenly realized that there was something familiar in the woman. She handed him a pink bag of restaurant sugar, and he immediately realized who it was.

"Are you still collecting this?" - the guest asked.

They sat in the kitchen, behind a small pine table. Bella leaned against the master's chair, bowed her head to the side, grumbling from time to time, and Monson, as usual, shoved a tasty piece, although Malin did not like that he was feeding the dog near the table. Hot cupcake melted in the tongue. And yet Monson could not take a sip.

He kept telling himself that it was great to see Vera Nielson after so many years, but he really couldn't be happy sincerely, and therefore he simply congratulated her mentally with the fact that she seemed to be doing well. But what is she doing here at his house? And why now?

To give himself time to think, Monson began to relate how he and his family returned here in 1984. He referred to the fact that Malin was offered a good job and that the children really wanted to go home; this, of course, was true, but Monson ignored the fact that Juhan and Yakub were persecuted at school. Other children mocked them, saying that their father is a useless policeman.

Then he turned to the events of the eighty-sixth: then they found colon cancer, he was treated and recovered. And he decided to lead a different lifestyle and change his profession.

"So you're not a cop anymore?" Vera asked, looking at him studyingly. Monson recognized this look right away, although he had last seen it many years ago.

- Not. I work in a leisure center. Here in Mjolby. Good job. Not meaningless.

He reached for another piece of cake - just not to look into her eyes. Bella energetically tailed the floor.

- Last year I went to early retirement and now - I'm doing home work now. Twice a week I take my grandchildren to kindergarten and bustle around Malin when she returns from work. We love to play golf.

He thoroughly bit off the cake. Without even having time to swallow, he felt his stomach protest.

"Well, what about you, Vera?"

"Veronica," she corrected. "I changed my name when I left home."

Monson listened to her story. Work, study abroad, lives in Stockholm, became a psychotherapist. I listened carefully, nodded and assented in the right places. But he was constantly disturbed by her striking resemblance to her mother.

Cupcake was already cold, and Bella ran to her basket when they spoke of Billy. Monson managed to gather his thoughts. He prepared standard answers, such as those that he had given out to particularly persistent journalists: the police considered Billy's case to be solved, and although he, Monson, of course, was disappointed that he had not reached the trial of the criminal, he nevertheless left everything in the past a long time ago.

He told the guest all this and something else, trying to make the words sound sincere and convincing. And at the same time he watched the expression on her face. I looked for signs of anger or a desire to blame him. To his relief, he saw nothing of the kind. Veronica only smiled slightly and nodded sympathetically several times, so Monson decided that the danger had passed. I was relieved to note that I was worried in vain that she had not come here to call him to account.

And then Veronica asked a question that took him by surprise.

"Do you think Tommy Root really killed my brother?" She asked softly. That's all, but Monson made a journey through time in a split second. Back to Skane, in the Rafting, that damn summer.

Chapter 48

1983 summer

He was standing in the back yard of the police station. Streetlights had already been lit, but the one that was supposed to illuminate the courtyard was not working, and the entrance to the prison was drowned in the darkness. It was stuffy, a thunderstorm was approaching. Lightning flashed on the horizon.

Monson held Roth's keychain. He put his finger in the ring and twisted it. One key to the pump room, two to some kind of door to the courtyard. The fourth - from the red "Amazon", the car stood right there, a little at a distance, at the fence. There was also a fragment of a roe deer horn in a bundle, in which Root drilled two holes. The horn was brilliant, it was polished by the neighboring keys and hard fingers of the owner. At the end of the horn dangled the fifth key; neither Monson nor city investigators could determine which lock he was unlocking.

Monson once again began to consider this typical faceless key. This can come up to any kind of hanging castle, as Bure and Borg pointed out to him. In a way, they were right when they said that people always keep keys. They found a whole bunch in the house, let Monson try them all, please, they don't mind. Unless, of course, in the midst of a murder investigation, he wants to focus on the keys.

Monson understood what they meant. And yet something in this unidentified vein haunted him. Root used the other keys from this bunch daily. Important keys that he decided to always carry with him. And he also attached a makeshift keychain to the key to the padlock, as if to highlight it. That should mean something. Just a must.

The prisoner's doors opened, and Tommy Root stepped out of there. He carried a plastic bag with his belongings; pulled out a cigarette, put it in his mouth. Monson silently watched him. He was glad that he did not succumb to the urge to beat the detainee. Maybe he is a useless policeman, the city is right in this, but still not so bad.

Root lit a cigarette, stopped next to him and took a drag. He blew smoke to the side. Monson automatically watched a cloud of smoke, and it seemed to him that something was moving in the dark window of the police station. Probably, some of the employees could not resist and spy now on how the unthinkable happens: they release the killer of the child.

- I beg. Monson held out a bunch of keys, holding the one from the padlock between his thumb and forefinger. When Root reached for the bundle, Monson did not let her go.

- This one from which castle?

- I do not remember. - Root shrugged. His voice was indifferent, as if the question did not seem to him important at all. Still, Monson was sure: Root was lying.

Root made an effort and looked into the policeman's eyes; a wry smile of a man who is trying to pass off a lie as truth. Monson continued to glare at him, trying to think of anything to bring Roth back to his cell. Avoid waiting for him, Monson, defeat and contempt.

The first drops of rain fell on the asphalt. Root was still calmly smiling.

- So can I go?

Monson reluctantly released the keys from his hands.

"You're still a suspect, Tommy." Do not leave the village, hear?

Monson stood and watched Root rush to his car. I watched as the Amazon, screeching with wipers, leaves the gate. Raindrops streamed down the temples and neck. Monson pinched the skin on his stomach and twisted it until the pain replaced the other senses.

Thunder boomed again. Deaf, hateful thunder that seemed to creep over the village. The monster that has just been released.

Chapter 49

- I stood in the courtyard of the police station and looked Rota in the eye. It seems I imagined that evil could be seen in them. Or hoped to see something else. Blame, remorse. Hint that everything was a mistake, a silly drunken trick that failed. - Monson was silent, looking down at his own hands.

"But you didn't see any of this?" Veronica asked softly.

Monson shook his head, twisting the engagement ring.

He was thinner than she remembered. His hair thinned noticeably, which, however, is not surprising, he is still more than sixty. But in the main, Monson has not changed. Pensive, capable of compassion. Good man.

Veronica felt his sadness as soon as he opened it to her. Over coffee, his sadness grew, although he did his best to convince Veronica that he had left Billy's business in the past. Now, talking about the evening, when he had to let go of Tommy Roth, he gave up. Monson's sadness depressed her just like her dad. Maybe because Monson and dad were alike, or because his sadness was close to her own.

"When you left the police ..." Veronica began and received a slow nod in response. "You said - because of illness ..." She paused, waited for him to raise his eyes. "But there was another reason, too?"

For a moment, it seemed to her that Monson would protest. Veronica raised an eyebrow, indicating that she wanted to hear the truth, not a defensive speech. She had resorted to this trick before and knew well that it did not always work. Fortunately, Monson reacted exactly as she expected. He lowered his eyes again, twisted the ring.

- I left because I could not stand it. I could not bear the realization that he released the killer Billy. I lay awake at night and chewed endlessly on the thought that I could do things differently. It's better. - He looked up. His eyes were blank. "Malin says the Billy affair ate me from the inside out, like cancer." And she is right.

Veronica nodded and paused, letting his sorrow widen.

"My brother Matthias is a cop in the Rafting, you know?" She asked.

- Yes, I heard. - Monson smiled faintly.

- Matthias re-read the investigation materials ten times, no less. He says no mistakes were made. What if he led the search for Billy, he would act just like you. - By the reaction of Monson, Veronica realized that he appreciated it; his eyes softened, and Veronica moved on to the real purpose of her visit.

"What if everything is completely wrong?" - she said. "What if Billy is alive?"

She told Monson everything. She began with Isak showing up in her group, telling about a trip home, about Sailor's words and about his find made in Askedalen.

How nice it was to talk to someone who was familiar with the case, but still saw it from the side. With someone who did not try to interrupt her, pointing out awkward details and immediately dismissing her theories. Monson dealt with surprise and listened very carefully.

Veronica was sure: the key on Roth's bundle, which Monson had just talked about, goes to the lock she found near the caisson. Monson agreed with her, noting that this explains why Root kept the key on the key and why he lied about it. In addition, the fragment of the horn on which the key was hanging seemed to be of the same artisanal production as the scary "breeze" in the hunting hut.

But something still did not dock. If Root rushed to Askedalen right after he was released, and immediately hid a caisson with guns and a threatening letter in the thicket, then why was the castle cut off? Did Root himself clean the caisson, or had someone else done this earlier? Someone who knew about the caisson and its contents, but who did not have a key? In this case, the only suspect was Sailor.

Monson did not agree with this.

- Sailor was a drunkard, who mostly hung around the pubs. He, coupled with some idiot, managed to drown the boat in the marl pit when we were everywhere looking for Billy. I just don't believe that Sailor would be tired of cleansing Tommy Root. If he did this, then certainly not on his own initiative. And Root was in the cell, they didn't let anyone in, so he could not give Sailor instructions. Monson scratched his neck thoughtfully. "Besides, I strongly doubt that Root would trust Sailor." Tommy Root was smart and cunning. Using Sailor as a henchman during poaching raids or even telling him to shoot a window in your uncle's car is one thing. But making him an accomplice in kidnapping is another. Unnecessary risk ...

Monson frowned, got up and brought the coffee pot.

"But if the caisson was not devastated by Root or Sailor, then who?" - Veronica asked when he filled both cups. "Could Roth have another accomplice?"

- It is possible. - Monson sipped his coffee.

Now he looked completely different. His back straightened, his voice hardened; Monson now looked a bit like Matthias. Veronica found herself smiling.

"If your theory is correct ..." Monson said thoughtfully. "If Isak is Billy, then someone cared for him while Root was in prison." He fed, watered, looked after him so that he would not get hurt, he would not get sick.

- Nilla Root? Maybe she?

- Not. We thought that Billy was hidden in the pump room, where Root was carving carcasses.

- Why?

Monson grimaced, making it clear that he would gladly have avoided details.

"There were handcuffs and an old bed." - He, looking for a reaction, squinted at Veronica.

And she did not disappoint - she nodded silently, offering to continue, although inside her everything was cold.

- If Nilla Root was involved, she would not talk about the pumping room. In addition, she had her own children, and the boy is the same age as Billy. I can hardly believe that she would have done something like that.

"And how did Root explain the handcuffs and the bed?"

How busy she sounded to her! Monson, too, seems surprised - he raised his chin.

- At first he did not say anything, and then, when they gave him a lawyer, he began to claim that he had met women there. Married women whose names he did not want to disclose. Yes, such rumors circulated about him, but his whole story sounded like an essay, which the lawyer helped him to concoct. - Monson drank some more coffee.

"But no matter who the unknown accomplice or accomplice was, he or she should have taken Billy out of the pump room when it became clear that Roth had been arrested. And a week later, when he was released, he took Billy and fled south, "Veronica summed up.

"More than possible," Monson nodded.

- Well then? What happened then? And why did Roth need to take Billy away?

- Here it is worth considering.

Monson and a cheerful dog led her to the door. After hesitating, Veronica hugged Monson goodbye. He smelled of cupcake and Old Spice. Monson hugged her in response, promised to think about the case and said that Veronica could call him whenever he wanted. He said as if he really wanted her to call.

Chapter 50

The city is a place for those whose real home is somewhere else, but they don't know where exactly yet. Veronica read it in a book or maybe heard on TV. There is something in this statement. She herself lived in Paris, London, Berlin, and now in Stockholm. And in none of these cities did she feel truly at home.

In the last hours, while driving a car, she thought a lot about Christer Monson. About how he talked with love about his wife, about children and grandchildren, whose photos hung on the walls of the hallway and living room. Monson was married to Malin, probably thirty-five years old, no less, but he was still looking forward to her coming home. Veronica lacked this - she had no one to wait for. She had no one at all.

Veronica opened the front door, carefully listening to the dark depths of the apartment. It was quiet and motionless. Veronica lit up the whole world and did not calm down until she looked into the pantry and under the bed. The apartment looked like Veronica had left her, nothing indicated that anyone had been here. Veronica opened the window to ventilate the rooms, looked out and looked at the end of the street. There was no smoker. But the night butterflies are back. They circled around their electric sun, repeating the same mistake.

The phone winked at her from the kitchen table. Four winks, by the number of posts. First, the two when the caller breathed and hung up. The third message also began with silence, but when she already wanted to move on to the next, a voice was heard.

"This is Lars again, from the group." - Lars muttered incoherently - apparently, he was drunk. - You did not call back. Damn ... - He hesitated, something inaudibly mumbled, and the message ended. Veronica never understood where his number came from. We need to discuss this with Ruud tomorrow.

Matthias left the fourth message:

- Hello! It's me. I wanted to check that you got there normally. Well and ... - Veronica felt like he squirmed. "I was glad to see you, Vera." We should see each other more often. - Another pause. "No, that's all." Take care of yourself, "he finished hastily. Judging by his voice, Matthias was dissatisfied with himself, as if he wanted to say something else, more substantial.

Veronica turned off the answering machine. I looked at the light bulb - it was now burning with a steady red light. No one else called her.

She pressed the saved message button. The last news from Leon was here, and this time Veronica listened to it from the very beginning.

"This is the end, Veronica. How do you not understand? I do not want more letters. I do not want messages or conversations in the middle of the night. And stop waiting for me at the entrance. This is already a disease. - He sighed. - Enough, Veronica. I beg you. Enough. "

Chapter 51

"Christer, are you sleeping?" Malin's voice took Monson by surprise. For half an hour he silently lay in the dark; meanwhile, the clock left midnight behind. His wife's breathing became deeper, and Monson let go of his thoughts.

- Sorry, I was just lying, thinking about something. I woke you up?
- Not.

He knew that it was not true, that his wife had lied so that he would not feel guilty. She should get up early tomorrow morning. Monson felt her turn to him and held out his hand to rest her head on his shoulder.

"Is it because of Vera Nilson?" Asked Malin.

"Veronica," he muttered.

- What?

"Her name is Veronica Lind now." Veronica, not Vera.

"Yes, you did." Why do you think she changed her name?

He patted Malin on the back.

- I do not know. Maybe she wanted to run away from the past.

"But she doesn't want to anymore."

- It seems so.

"Do you think her version is true?" Well, is Billy Nilson alive?

"If you asked me a few years ago, I would say no." But I saw Veronica, listened to her story - and now I don't know. What if it is? Root could take Billy out of the village, leave him with someone or take care of him. But then the question arises - why? Why did he abandon his own family to take care of someone else's child?

It was quiet for a few seconds. Malin continued to stroke his chest. Monson liked it, liked that his wife was nearby.

"What can you do, Christer?" What can you do to help Veronica get to the bottom of the truth?

- I don't know yet. Maybe try to find out what happened to Roth's wife and children? Suddenly, Tommy let one of them know about himself. Maybe they know something that will help us move on.

"Good," Malin muttered in his ear. "And now that you have come to this thought, let's sleep, huh?"

My love

I once wanted summer, warmth and a blue sky to last forever. Then I longed for autumn - autumn will come, and you will take me away from here.

How did such a stupidity come to my mind to imagine that you and I have a future? There is no coolness, no mercy - only eternal torment under the ruthless sun, and then darkness and cold will swallow us.

I can no longer keep our secret. We made a mistake, now I know that. Payback awaits us.

Chapter 52

The heat was the same as the day before. Veronica took a shower for a long time, then dressed, as usual: a white shirt, black pants. Neutral and businesslike, as a person who takes his work extremely seriously.

She took the metro to the Community Center, where she was met by Ruud, who seemed to be in a good mood. He hugged her, said he was glad to see. They went into his office. Chairs in the hall stood in a circle. As soon as they saw them, Veronica felt how anticipation awakens in her. She squinted at the chair closest to the door. She imagined Isak sitting on it.

In the study, Ruud said with some complacency how he fought for her. As the personnel department convinced that that Saturday phone call was an isolated event. And the lanky Bengt also helped. He said that Veronica gives the impression of a collected person and recognizes his mistake.

"Bengt wants you to come to him a few more times, to be sure." Asks to make an appointment in the coming days.

Ruud spoke as if personally responsible for her behavior. It was slightly annoying, but Veronica was silent. I just signed on the forms Ruud put in front of her.

"You spent the weekend in Skane," Ruud said when they finished. "It's good there in the summer." Native places? In your speech is not noticeable.

"Well ..." Veronica forced a smile. "I left when I was eighteen." Not shelving, as they say.

She took a deep breath, hoping that the sigh would not sound strange and that Ruuda would not want to delve further into her life.

- Here's how. And why?

Actually it meant: what did you want to run away from?

"Why not especially," Veronica lied. - Village life is not for me. They say two types of people grow up in a village. Those who stay and those who leave.

"That's how it is," Ruud repeated. - And you are from the second? Of those who leave?

Made in the USA
Middletown, DE
22 February 2020